Newton
and the
Giant

Newton and the Giant

Michael McGowan

HarperTrophyCanada™

An imprint of HarperCollinsPublishersLtd

Newton and the Giant

Published by HarperTrophyCanada™, an imprint of HarperCollins Publishers Ltd

First trade paperback edition by HarperTrophyCanada™,
an imprint of HarperCollins Publishers Ltd: 2003.
This mass market edition: 2005

HarperCollins books may be purchased for educational, business,
or sales promotional use through our Special Markets Department.

HarperTrophyCanada™ is a trademark of HarperCollins Publishers

HarperCollins Publishers Ltd
2 Bloor Street East, 20th Floor
Toronto, Ontario, Canada
M4W 1A8

www.harpercollins.ca

Library and Archives Canada Cataloguing in Publication

McGowan, Michael, 1966–
Newton and the giant /
Michael McGowan ; Shelagh McNulty, illustrator. – 1st mass market ed.

ISBN 0-00-639258-X

I. McNulty, Shelagh II. Title.

PS8575.G663N48 2005 jC813′.6 C2004-906620-X

OPM 9 8 7 6 5 4 3 2 1

Printed and bound in the United States
Set in Monotype Joanna

To my family,
especially Shelagh, Henry, Wiley, and Frances
(and also to Joey, who kept asking for more chapters)

Chapter 1

Newton's socks were soaked. His feet were prunes. And he hadn't even been put in the game yet.

To be outside on such a day was insanity. But somehow the school continually got away with forcing its students to participate in sports. The leaves were almost off the trees and winter was loudly knocking at the door. Newton sat on the bench and shivered and felt his forehead for symptoms of fever. His nose was raw, signaling a cold, potentially pneumonia, which would mean doctors, hospitals, needles and an extended recovery indoors. He tried to hawk up something solid for visual confirmation, but so far his pipes were clean. Probably by bedtime his snot would be radioactive green, his illness so severe that someday entire medical books would be dedicated to detailing the disease.

Coach Henley turned and looked at his players on the sidelines. Newton tried to make himself invisible—he had read that if you concentrated hard enough, disappearing was possible. During the first half of the game he had tried unsuccessfully to make Coach Henley disappear. This time, he thought only about himself, willing, wishing invisibility. After all, he had no idea how soccer worked and refused to try to learn. A ball, a bunch of sweaty kids, hyperactive parents and a ruthless, foul-tempered coach.

No, soccer was not for him.

"Wiggins," Coach bellowed, "get in the game! It's a league rule!"

"But, Coach, I'm—"

"Wiggins! In!! And not one more word out of you!" Newton could see almost all the way around Coach's eyeballs, they were that far out of their sockets.

"Coach, I'm—"

"Wiggins!"

Newton had no choice. He trudged onto the field, avoiding puddles.

The game moved in a blur. Newton watched people he knew and respected—McNulty, Smith, Fox, Solomon, Gregg—chasing the ball, furiously getting knocked to the ground, only to haul themselves up and dive in for more action. Wet, dirty and bruised, they seemed to be enjoying the activity immensely.

Out on the field, Newton's strategy was to avoid the action at all costs. But as hard as he tried to do this, Newton occasionally found himself in the middle of the melee. And with the score tied 1–1, in the dying seconds of the contest, moments before Newton would be released from this ordeal, the ball came at him. Of course, at that moment, Newton was busy calculating design specifications for his latest invention: wings. He had been secretly working on this project for the past month. As a result, he didn't know where he was on the field and he didn't care. Why was the ball here? Didn't everybody understand that he had no interest in it?

Most times, Newton simply would have turned and headed the other way, but for some reason, perhaps out of spite, perhaps because of the irritating yelling coming from the sidelines, he decided to kick the ball. With all his might (and in spite of his ill health) he connected foot to leather.

And even Newton admired the well-executed effort. The ball shot away in a direction that was more or less as intended, miraculously sailing toward the top corner of the net.

The goalie lunged for it but was too late!

The ball went in! The ball went in!

The referee's whistle announced the end of the game.

His teammates were on their feet, amazed that Newton had done the impossible.

And for a moment, Newton could feel the faintest appeal for the activity. Perhaps, just maybe, soccer actually *was* for him.

This was immediately replaced with disgust.

Not his own, but that of his teammates and especially Coach Henley.

"Wiggins, you idiot!" Coach yelled. "You kicked the ball into *our net!*"

And then Newton realized his awful mistake—a mistake that could not be undone.

Coach Henley was twelve shades of angry. "How could you do this to me? Our perfect record is over!"

"Because I hate soccer!" Newton yelled back

without really thinking. Perhaps because deep down he wanted to make Coach Henley believe he did it on purpose (even though he didn't, of course).

Everyone—on both teams—looked at Newton with awe and amazement. Parents were shocked. Little brothers and sisters, though they may not have understood, knew something important had happened. In the history of soccer matches no one could recall a kid purposely kicking the ball into his own net. Newton started off the field, pretending not to notice the stares.

"Wiggins, you miscreant, get over here, ASAP!" Coach Henley yelled.

Newton stopped, looked at the coach and shouted, "No!" and kept going toward his bike.

Later, when he learned that they had to cart Coach Henley off the field on a stretcher because of the heart attack, Newton felt some responsibility . . . but was able to dismiss it as Coach's problem, not his.

That night, at 228 Bessborough Drive, dinner was miserable. It was Newton against his family.

Not one of them had ever met a sport he or she didn't love, and they devoted an entire room to displaying all of their trophies, medals and ribbons. In their youth, his parents had been champion sprinters, expert golfers, fearless hockey players. Countless times Newton had been reminded that he had yet to contribute a single prize to the room. Nothing, not even a participation ribbon or a good sportsman certificate. But that was only because his quadruplet brothers—Engelbert, Ernest, Eric and Earl—had refused to acknowledge his Science Fair awards. Not only had Newton won the overall District Prize for the past three years (for a buried treasure locator, an automatic homework completer and a solar-powered ice-cream maker), but also the trophies were huge—even bigger than the one Earl got at tae kwon do.

"Let me get this straight," his father said, trying his best to be kind and understanding, but completely baffled. "You kicked the ball into your own net?"

His mother took short breaths, trying to calm herself. "Not that it matters, but the quadruplets tell me we're the laughing stock of town—not to mention the fact that Coach Henley is in the hospital."

Newton knew it did matter to his mother. To her, reputations meant something.

Earl piped in. "It's true, Mom. If I were you, just to be safe, I wouldn't go outside for a few days."

"It might make the national news," Ernest added.

"But I told you, I never even wanted to play soccer in the first place. It's a stupid game," Newton said, and immediately wished he hadn't.

The group went silent.

Mouths fell open. Half-chewed food could be seen.

The quadruplets stopped talking for the first time since Newton could remember. Eight dark, menacing eyes stared at him. The hair on their four red heads seemed to be standing at angry attention. The spray of freckles across their noses glowed irritably.

They suddenly seemed a whole head (instead of a half-head) taller than Newton. Engelbert, the oldest of the quadruplets by six minutes and thirty-three seconds, and the toughest by half a biceps, muttered just loud enough so only Newton could hear, "We'll deal with you after dinner."

Newton gulped. A threat from Engelbert was bad bordering on completely and utterly disastrous.

The quadruplets were twelve, two years older than Newton. As far as Newton was concerned, they might as well have been aliens the way they communicated with each other in a secret language. Because they were so good at sports, they never got in trouble for blowing up toys, torturing animals or pushing grandmothers into snowbanks. Adults seemed blind to the obvious fact that they were the meanest kids in the neighborhood. Especially Newton's parents. Whenever they got bored, which happened frequently because they had extremely short attention spans, the quadruplets would devise ways to bug their younger brother. Once they stole all his Christmas presents and replaced them with packages of mud. Another time they hung him by the ankles from the jungle gym, trying to make him say "uncle"—until he barfed.

To make matters worse, his parents believed

everything that the quadruplets told them. Newton's theory was that the quadruplets were so awesome at sports that his parents had concluded they were perfect in every other way as well. They couldn't imagine their star athlete sons behaving in ways that were less than sportsmanlike. As a result, for Newton, complaining about some injustice the quadruplets had dealt him was pointless. His brothers would deny everything and of course his parents would believe them, no matter how much evidence suggested otherwise. Newton couldn't really blame his parents. Just like horses, they had a rather large blind spot—theirs was for the quadruplets. In most other ways (hugs, kisses, bedtime tuck-ins) they passed parenting with top marks.

Except for cooking. That night dessert was an unidentifiable glob of pink that had a strong hint of dishwasher detergent in it. Newton's mother called it *parfait*. Newton was having a hard time even getting it close to his mouth. How could his mother be the world's worst cook? No one else in the family ever seemed to notice, but his best friend Max certainly agreed.

Newton's father turned to Engelbert and announced, "Your mother and I are going salsa dancing this evening. Do you mind baby-sitting the kids?"

Engelbert pretended to think about it for a couple of seconds before answering, "Why, Father, not at all." He turned to Newton, slyly smiled, then said, "This dessert is scrumptious. Newton, could you please pass the bowl over so I might have a third helping?"

Newton had barely pulled up the rope to the attic and put the cover over the opening (fortunately located in his bedroom) when he heard his mother's instructions—"You children behave"—and then the awful *thud* of the front door shutting. His parents wouldn't be home until eight, and Newton would have to remain hidden for two hours if he had any hope of staying alive. The moment his brothers found him, without adult supervision, who knows what they would do.

From downstairs Earl yelled through their father's bullhorn, "YOU CAN RUN, NEWTON, AND YOU CAN HIDE, BUT WE'LL HUNT YOU DOWN AND WHEN WE FIND YOU, YOU'LL REGRET THE DAY YOU DECIDED TO SCORE ON YOUR OWN NET."

Ernest grabbed the bullhorn to add, "COME OUT NOW. MAKE IT EASY ON YOURSELF!"

Eric piped in, "THE LONGER WE SPEND LOOKING FOR YOU, THE MORE IT'S GOING TO HURT."

Engelbert apparently had nothing to say. Which was the most frightening of all.

Newton had brought with him the portable phone, a flashlight, a stack of comics and a jar of peanut butter. The phone in case he got desperate and was forced to call the police to help rescue him, the flashlight so he could read the comics, and the peanut butter so he wouldn't starve to death if his parents never made it back from salsaing.

To those skilled in the hiding arts, the attic may seem like the choice of a novice. Wouldn't that be one of the first places seekers as skilled as the quadruplets would look? But Newton's attic was different. Along the front wall, behind the boxes of unused toys, Meccano sets, short-wave radio components and outgrown clothes was a small red door barely big enough for Newton to squeeze through (he hoped), but definitely too small for his brothers. What was behind it and why the door was there at all Newton had no idea.

With his parents out dancing and his brothers on a mission, it was a door that Newton hoped would save his life. The only problem—and Newton even hated to admit this to himself—was that he was a little scared. Truth be told, the door frightened the kneecaps off him. On an exploration mission three Sundays ago, Newton and his best friend Max had first discovered the door. Even then, they had voted not to open it. Though there was nothing about the door to distinguish it as particularly terrifying, Max was pretty sure ogres were behind it, and Newton was convinced a couple of witches were using it as a hideout. Since then Newton had often thought about the door. But he had never been brave enough to venture that deep into the attic again.

Newton heard Ernest and Engelbert enter his room.

"That little twerp's up there. I just know it," said Ernest.

"Shh!" said Engelbert, and he started smelling the air. Engelbert had a nose so sensitive that simply by sniffing he could tell what hockey players were on the cards even before the pack was opened. "Peanut butter. We're close."

Newton put his hand on the handle of the red door. It felt cold and gave off the slightest of electrical charges. Newton hesitated. He tried to talk himself into bravery by whispering, "Wiggins, this is a life or death situation." At any moment Ernest and Engelbert would force open the hatch and rush into the attic. Still, he could not bring himself to open the door.

"The attic, he's in the attic," Engelbert declared.

Newton shuddered.

Ernest got on the bullhorn. "NEWTON IS IN THE ATTIC! I REPEAT, CODE WHITE! NEWTON IS IN THE ATTIC! RENDEZVOUS IN NEWTON'S ROOM AND AWAIT FURTHER INSTRUCTIONS!"

Within seconds Newton knew his four brothers were standing on his bed, directly underneath the hatch, staring up.

For a moment Newton considered simply coming out and taking his punishment—whatever that might be. But he thought about how his soccer goal was an honest mistake and how sports really were stupid and how unfair it was that he had been out on the muddy field in the first place and how he didn't care if he had embarrassed his family and how they never would have believed him anyway if he just told them the truth about the goal. . .

The cover to the opening started to move.

Realizing he had only seconds to spare, Newton

took a deep breath and opened the mysterious door.

Engelbert, closely followed by his brothers, was faster than Newton had anticipated and was up and in the attic instantaneously.

"There he is!"

"Quick! Get him!"

"COME OUT WITH YOUR HANDS UP!" Ernest shouted in the bullhorn.

Engelbert plowed through the boxes like they were empty and flew at Newton's feet.

Newton still had enough time to squeeze through the door, except . . . it was smaller than he had calculated! He was only halfway wiggling through when he felt Engelbert's cold hands on his ankles, trying to tug him back.

This was bad. Newton was nowhere near as strong as Engelbert. How would he ever make it? Nonetheless he tried, valiantly straining even his eyelids in the effort. He thrashed his feet and wormed and squirmed for all he was worth. But Engelbert hung on, clamped to Newton's legs like bubblegum to a desk.

Slowly, inch by inch, Engelbert dragged Newton back into the room.

"That's the way! Don't let him go!" Ernest yelled.

"Hang on!" Earl screamed.

"You're the man!" Eric added.

Newton desperately clung to the other side of the door though he was nearly all the way back out. His muscles ached. His arms felt like they were stretched to orangutan length. Even his fingernails were sweating.

But he knew that no matter how hard he tried, how much he grunted and groaned, it was hopeless. Engelbert would eventually haul him out and his brothers would torture him and he would never even be able to enjoy his summer vacation, which was only seven months away.

The urge to let go and simply accept his fate was overwhelming. But one look at Engelbert's face and Newton knew he must hold on.

Engelbert pulled.

Newton clung.

And suddenly Newton felt hands on his wrists pulling him back toward the door. Strong, large hands. He turned and tried to see who or what it was that was pulling him, but there were only shadows. Was it witches? Ogres? Or something else altogether more terrifying? All he knew was that whatever had him was strong—stronger than Engelbert. Newton was terrified of Engelbert winning the tug-of-war but more terrified of the unknown force pulling him through the door.

The tide turned. Newton was going in the opposite direction, back through the door. First his shoulders, then his stomach, next his hips.

Engelbert was outraged to be losing the battle because Engelbert never lost at anything. In fact, he was on a winning streak that had started when he was the first to plop out of the womb. "You're cheating, Newton!" he yelled, and yanked on Newton's legs with even more fury.

Newton felt like he was being torn in two and wondered how much blood and gross intestines there would be if his legs ripped off.

However, in spite of Engelbert's efforts, it was no use. Newton's knees, then feet, went through the opening.

"I'm never letting go!" Engelbert croaked, but he had no choice.

Newton had escaped! (At least Engelbert's clutches . . .)

No sooner had Engelbert let go than the door started to close. Before it shut completely, Engelbert shouted, "We'll be waiting for you! This is not over! No one messes with the Force of Four and survives! Prepare to face our wrath!" The quadruplets pounded and they banged, but for all their anger they couldn't open the door.

Soon enough they'd return with power tools.

Newton sat very still for a couple of minutes trying to get his bearings. Whoever or whatever had pulled him to the other side had let go. The room was so black, Newton could smell the darkness. He certainly couldn't see and his flashlight had gone AWOL. Who had pulled him in and where was this . . . thing?

"Hello?" Newton whispered nervously. "Is anybody here?" His voice echoed and the room seemed much bigger than he thought could be possible.

No one answered.

"Hello." Newton tried again. "I really appreciate what you did for me." Still no answer. Newton felt for the door but could not find it.

What was this place? Why had nobody told him about it before?

Newton crawled on the floor, searching with his hands, trying to locate a light switch, his flashlight, anything that would illuminate the situation. He crawled and crawled, all the while expecting to bump into something truly dreadful. A dead body. Slugs. A bucket of blood. But he felt nothing. Newton had no idea how far he had gone or how long he had been in the room but it seemed like an eternity and he was scared. Did vampires hang out here? Ghosts? Ghouls?

Panic slithered over him like a snake and Newton crawled faster. He shouted out for his brothers, the echoes rebounding into frightening howls. Still no one answered. How long would the quadruplets wait to tell their parents where Newton had gone? Why had he been so stupid to venture into here in the first place?

He was almost whimpering when he heard something metallic hit the ground. His flashlight! Of course, he had put it in his pocket. Quickly Newton turned it on.

It would have been better to stay in the dark.

Newton would have screamed but fright had a stranglehold on his voice cords.

He switched the light off, then on again to make sure his brain was fully operational.

It was.

Caught in the weak beam were two puss-filled eyes, mere inches from Newton's own peepers.

Attached to the eyes was a face, the biggest and ugliest Newton had ever seen. The skin looked like the bark of a tree and moles dotted its landscape. Black hairs flared out of the nostrils. The lips were scabby, with drool spilling from the left side onto a raw, red chin.

The creature definitely was big enough to be a giant. Then again, maybe it was part ogre. Or could it be a troll? What if it was something even more gruesome? Newton wished he had brought his *Field Guide to Scary Creatures* with him, but more important, he wished he had never decided to open the door to this awful place.

Chapter 2

The creature stood up and pulled a switch. The room was revealed in a dim green light. Though it was bigger than an airport hangar, apart from the thick vines growing on the walls and ceiling, the space stood empty. Because Newton only came up to the creature's shins, he had a very good view of two enormous feet—which looked more reptilian than human. The three toenails of each foot were brown and needed to be cut; the skin was dry and leathery with deep cracks and appeared somewhat scaly. A purple vein popped from his left ankle and pulsated menacingly.

"All right, young man, where do I go? Quick. Quick. I've been rudely delayed here for the better part of a lunar cycle and I'm not in any kind of mood to be trifled with. Show me the way and then be off with you, you pathetic shrimp," the creature said, his voice wavering between a deep boom and croaking high notes.

Newton looked up. Finally he managed to sputter, "Wh-wh-who are y-y-you?"

The creature scooped up Newton, brought him level with his face and shouted, "Who am I?"

Caught between crooked teeth were fleshy bits of unidentifiable gunk. Newts? Gnomes? Children? A wave of gross breath assaulted Newton, a smell so foul his eyes watered and the little glob of skin at the back of his throat quivered.

"I am Herbert, king of the giants, ruler of the giants, lord of the giants, most famous of all the giants, and of course, best looking of the giants." He paused, trying to think of something else, then added, "Want to hear me roar?"

"Well . . . no," Newton said.

"Egad! Are you certain? Absolutely positive?"

"I'm positive."

Herbert let out a disappointed but deep sigh, and Newton barely managed to avoid barfing. "Could you please put me down. I think I might be sick."

"Oh, dear. Don't be sick on me. Do you have any idea how much this suit cost? It's spun from the finest fabrics." Herbert's suit was torn and stained and pocked with holes and certainly didn't look expensive, but maybe that was the fashion where he lived.

Before putting Newton down, Herbert sniffed his socks and muttered, "Too fresh."

"What's too fresh?" Newton asked.

"Nothing," Herbert said quickly.

Back on the ground Newton felt much better.

Suddenly a telephone rang.

At first Newton couldn't figure out why there was a phone in this place, until he saw the flashing lights of the portable hanging out of his pocket and remembered. "Excuse me," he said to Herbert, and he answered the phone. "Hello?"

Max was on the line. "Hey, it's me. I heard about the soccer game. That's pretty cool. I wish I had been there. Good news. The doctors say Coach Henley will be out of the hospital in a month."

Herbert stared at Newton. Though he was very good at staring contests, Newton had to look away. "Um, Max, I'm sort of in the middle of something. You mind if I call you back?"

"Sure, Newton. What time? You know my number, right?"

"Max, you're my best friend. I know your number."

"Okay, okay. Just checking. What time?"

Ernest, who must have picked up the phone in their parents' bedroom, used the bullhorn to shout into the extension, "I DON'T KNOW HOW YOU MANAGED TO KEEP THAT DOOR LOCKED, BUT WE'RE COMING AFTER YOU, CHEEZE WHIZ!" then immediately hung up.

"Newton, is he serious? Please don't tell me you went into—"

But Newton never heard the rest of what Max had to say because Herbert grabbed the portable, shoved it in his mouth and started munching away. When he burped, a tiny whiff of smoke came out.

Newton couldn't believe he ate the phone. "What's wrong with you?"

"I'm famished, that's what's wrong with me," Herbert replied. "What else did you bring to eat?" Newton took out his jar of peanut butter, and Herbert flicked his tongue and licked the jar right out of Newton's hand, sliming his palm with a streak of black gob—perhaps the most disgusting thing Newton had experienced since the time he mistakenly ate a maggot.

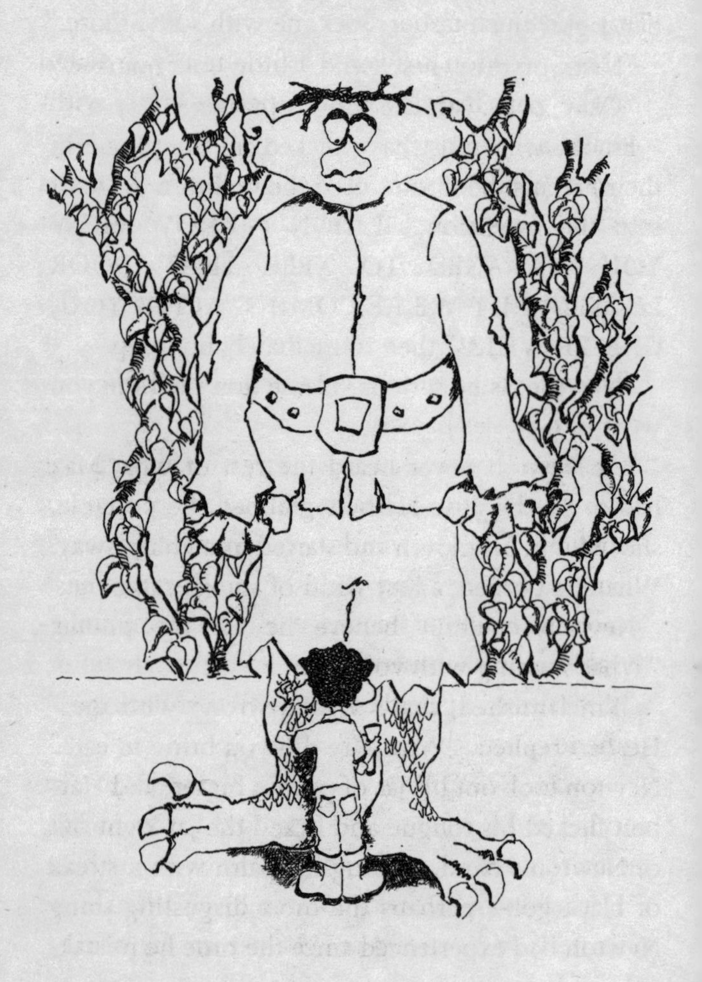

Herbert smacked his scaly lips. "You're right. That was much tastier. Sock me with some more."

"No," Newton answered a little testily, irritated that the giant had downed his peanut butter without asking.

"Well then, scoot. Off you go. Fetch. I have a medical condition. I feel faint if I don't eat enough."

"Listen," Newton said, "I don't understand who you are or what you're doing in my attic, but I've had a crappy day and the last thing I need right now is a giant with a bad attitude."

"I should never have pulled you through the door. What was I thinking? You're clearly not something I'd ever want to eat." Herbert yawned, then continued, "And the last thing someone as important as myself needs to do is waste my unbelievably valuable time listening to an utterly pointless, vertically challenged kid. So slither back to the pathetic existence you call a life."

Newton was furious. "All right, you freak, make another short-person comment and I start pulling leg hairs."

Herbert stepped back and muttered, "What is the primate world coming to," before loudly adding,

"I am royalty and will be treated accordingly. Where's the exit?"

"The only way I know out of here is through the attic door. The way I came in!"

"No call for rudeness."

"You started it."

"You did."

"No. You did."

"You."

"You—"

Suddenly a huge bird appeared out of nowhere, landed on Herbert's shoulder and cawed three times.

"Oh dear," Herbert said. "Three o'clock. I'm late. I must go. I guess I won't find any here. Ah, there's the exit!" With that, the giant turned and started for the far end of the room, where an open door had appeared. His bounding steps shook the floor.

"Wait!" Newton called, but Herbert never even so much as turned for a parting glance.

A bright light shone from beyond the door, and Newton wondered where it led. He started after the giant with the intention of merely taking a peek, but as soon as Herbert exited through the door it began to close. If he had any chance of getting there before it shut completely, Newton would have to pick up the pace.

As much as Newton hated sprinting (it went against everything he stood for), curiosity compelled him. Arms pumping and legs flailing, Newton ran as fast as he could. The door continued to close and Newton sped up even more, convinced he was doing irreparable, life-threatening damage to his system. He had never run so fast. With less than a sliver of the door still open, Newton arrived, panting like a dog in a sauna.

If he had had time to sit around and debate whether or not he should do what he did, maybe Newton would have acted differently. But he didn't and so, without thinking, going on instinct, he squeezed through the opening. Barely. A second later and he would have been pulverized like a fly splatting against a windshield.

The door shut with an echo and then vanished, melting into the scenery in much the same way a Popsicle disappears into hot concrete. Newton, however, did not yet realize the door was gone because he was squinting, still adjusting to the brightness.

When Newton finally was able to open his eyes and look around he was amazed, flabbergasted, slightly dumbfounded and a good deal awestruck.

He was in a different world altogether!

Chapter 3

Newton gulped. He turned around to look for the door, but, of course, it wasn't there. His heart, already doing a pretty good impersonation of a SuperBall in a blender, sped up even more.

Where was he and why had his teacher never mentioned this place during Geography? It wasn't so much that things were remarkably different—just enormously, humongously bigger. Newton had landed in a clearing. Around him, trees, the tallest he had ever seen, climbed skyward, their trunks as wide as houses, their leaves blocking the sunlight.

Except for a faint scraping noise off in the distance,

there were no other sounds. Birds weren't chatting. Squirrels weren't arguing. The forest was eerily silent.

Newton looked around, hoping to see Herbert, but the giant had vanished. Without much else to do, Newton started in the direction of the scraping, hoping to find a tourist information center or a bus station to take him back home. Out of the clearing, among the trees, the air was cooler and felt a bit on the spooky side. Newton had a feeling that unseen eyes were monitoring him. He kept turning around, expecting to find someone or something lurking, but all that greeted him were more tree trunks. The ground was covered with a pink moss and was easy to walk on. Soon Newton could no longer see the clearing. The farther he ventured into the forest, the cooler it became, and Newton wished he were dressed a little more warmly. This seemed like exactly the kind of weather in which one could catch pneumonia or some other life-threatening virus.

From behind him, breaking the silence, came the sound of horses' hooves. The noise grew louder and louder until two huge stallions came roaring into view. Newton, awed by the ferocity of their galloping and the intensity with which they tore through the forest, quickly hid behind a massive tree.

At first Newton thought he had been spotted. The horses stopped abruptly, not ten feet from him. But his presence had not been discovered. Two giants, dressed completely in black, dismounted. Though one was taller, they were both enormous, hulking creatures with fins sticking out of their backs. From out of a saddlebag a large hunk of meat was removed, which the giants passed back and forth. Soon their faces were covered in grease and stray chunks of meat.

Between mouthfuls of food the taller one asked, "Do I really have to go through with this?"

"We've been over this a thousand times, Natas. *Yes! You! Do!* Father demands it. That way, without any opposition, we can conquer these fools so much more easily. Our fuel supplies are almost used up. Look around—what do you see?"

The one called Natas turned his thick neck. "Leaves . . . ?" he asked uncertainly.

The other one hit him over the head with a drumstick. "Trees! Trees, you idiot! Sometimes I wonder if we really are brothers. Think about all the wood we can burn! Can you imagine how hot it will be for years to come? All this wood will be ours! So stop complaining and let's get this over with."

"But why don't we just attack them? That would be so much fun. We haven't had a bloody battle in months. Peace is so boring."

"We can't attack them. We'd never win if they fought us in the trees. But if we're clever, if we do this right, they'll never know what hit them. We can secretly bring all our troops in. Then . . . conquer! *Conquer! Conquer!*"

"But have you seen Princess Gertrude? She's vile!"

"Well, you can't very well marry the cook, now, can you! Don't worry, it will only be for a short time. Think positively. When it's over, you can kill her any way you wish."

"Really?" Natas asked, a hint of a smile crawling across his face.

"Of course."

Somewhat relieved, the giant calmed down. "It will be awful. Can you imagine, a giant from the Kingdom of the Liveds marrying a pathetic creature from the Kingdom of the Merriwarts? They live in trees and barely meet the height requirements for giant status. The whole idea makes me itchy."

"So scratch. But remember this: When our

destiny has been fulfilled, when we crush the Merriwarts and make them our slaves, it will be your name, not mine, that people fear—you that people will kneel before," he said, then tossed his drumstick bone to the ground. "The feast is starting soon. We're already late. We must go."

With that, the brothers mounted their horses and rode off in the same direction as the scraping noise, disappearing as suddenly as they had appeared.

Newton debated what he should do. He had no desire to run into the "brothers grim" again, but couldn't figure out a better plan than to continue following the scraping, this time with considerably more caution.

So he got on his hands and knees (in case of sniper fire) and started crawling. He would never forgive himself if he got his head shot off because he was too lazy to go into commando mode. Still, he was careful to keep his nose out of the dirt—a certain breeding ground for viruses. Max would have been proud of his military tactics. Crab-like, Newton moved along the forest floor until he was at the base of a tree directly under the scraping noise. Maybe thirty feet in the air, much to Newton's surprise, was Herbert. He was scraping bark off the tree and putting it into a bag.

"Herbert!" Newton shouted.

The giant looked down. He blinked a couple of times, then scurried down the tree.

"Oh my, this is disasterville," Newton could hear Herbert moaning. "How in the name of squashed newts did a little twerp like you manage to find me? And what could you possibly want?"

"Herbert, I am so glad to see you! I followed you through the door—"

"Stop! I don't need to hear any more." Herbert started to nervously hop from one foot to the other, like he had to go to the bathroom. Newton wondered why a king like Herbert would be so worried. Weren't kings allowed to do whatever they wanted to?

"I've got to think. I've got to think—" Herbert was muttering to himself, but he was interrupted when, from even higher in the tree, somewhere in the leaves, came another voice.

"Herbert! Haul your droopy butt up here *now* or I'll whup you into last year!" Without another word Herbert scurried up the trunk and disappeared.

Newton was flummoxed. To make matters worse, the sun was setting and it would be dark soon. The thought of spending a night in the forest creeped Newton out enough that he began to climb.

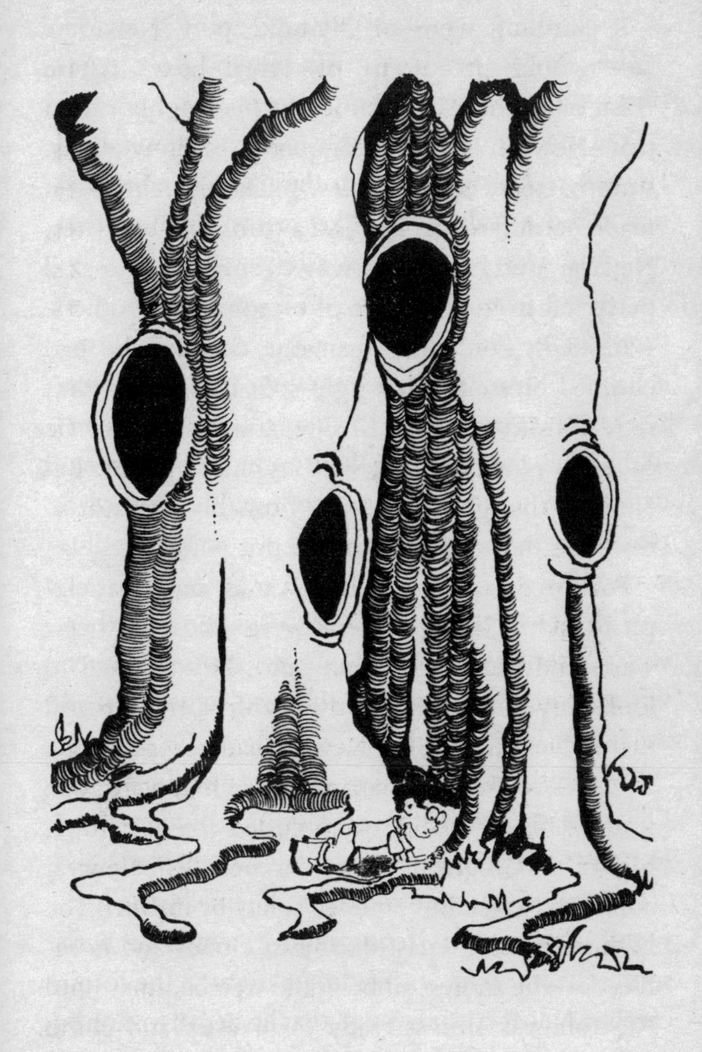

If climbing were an Olympic sport, Newton's face would already be on cereal boxes. There wasn't an arboreal specimen in his neighborhood that Newton hadn't conquered. Skinny trees, stumpy trees, oaks, maples, pines or walnuts—it made no difference. If it had a trunk and branches, Newton always found a way to spider up—a skill perfected from a lifetime of escaping his brothers. Admittedly, on more than one occasion he had climbed himself into a tight spot that he couldn't retreat from and the fire department had to be called to pluck him out with its cherry picker. But Newton thought that it was probably best not to dwell on those rare mishaps at this point.

For a tree so large, the bark was as smooth as elephant skin. Though there were folds, crevices, warts and pimples to grab onto, Newton had to look very hard to find them. Most trees reveal themselves quickly, but Newton had never met one so secretive. Still, he managed to inch upward, one strained fingernail and one curled toe at a time, higher and higher. When darkness fell Newton continued ascending, guided solely by instinct. The higher he went—past dizziness, clouds and nosebleeds—the more stubborn the tree became, until Newton was almost ready to give up and climb down. He had yet to reach a branch and his arms were shaky, his legs jiggled and, for the first time in his climbing career, he feared falling.

Fortunately, soon after that, a limb presented itself and then another and the climbing became easier. After another hour, Newton was nine-tenths exhausted when he thought he saw a light. But he blinked and then it was darkness again. For a moment Newton wondered if he was becoming unglued. Was he seeing some sort of mirage?

He was thankful when the wind picked up and parted the leaves and he saw the light again coming from directly above him. He hurried up three more branches and then scrambled along a limb that was as wide as a sidewalk. As he headed toward the large square of light, Newton soon realized that it was coming from a window. Music, yelling, laughing, and aromas so rich Newton could practically eat them filled the air.

It took Newton a couple of jumps but finally he was able to grab the sill of the large window and pull himself up.

Newton peered inside.

And discovered he was looking down at a huge hall, lit by hundreds of glowing snakes that had wrapped themselves around vines on the ceiling.

The snakes hummed like fluorescent lights. The hall was packed with giants who were elbow-to-elbow eating and dancing. At least, Newton *thought* it was dancing. A five-piece orchestra belted out tunes at a frenetic pace as the giants bopped up and down and slammed into each other. From Newton's vantage point they looked like bowling pins that refused to topple over. Along one wall were long tables piled with food, and Newton's stomach did somersaults just thinking about eating something.

The longer Newton looked, the more incredible the sights became. The mood was clearly festive, almost circus-like, with roars of laughter echoing off the rafters and wafting through the window. Newton noticed a crowd that had circled around a hunchbacked giant with a tiny pet dragon at his side. Various targets were set up and the dragon scorched them by shooting bolts of fire from its mouth. On the next table, five full-sized adult giants were being juggled by a young giantess who looked to be no more than a toddler, really. Newton wondered how she had the strength to keep them all in the air without being crushed to death. Another giant—the fattest Newton had ever seen (not that he had seen that many giants)—

floated above the crowd. Each time he opened his mouth a brightly colored egg would drop out and there would be a flurry of activity below, as others jostled to catch it.

But the most incredible sight of all was a giantess carrying her head under her arm like a football. From his perch on high, Newton could see the veins and goo on her neck where the head was supposed to rest. When the head wanted to talk, the giantess politely held it up so that other giants wouldn't be forced to bend down to make eye contact.

At the far end of the room, looking over the proceedings, sat a young giantess. Newton guessed she was somehow terribly important. She wore a dazzling jeweled crown and an elaborate gown embroidered with fancy stitching. But food was splotched across the front and her hair poked out of the crown in a most alarming manner. Even from across the confusion of the festivities, Newton could have sworn she looked terrifically bored.

An old, wrinkled giant stood up and moved toward the giantess. Wisps of white hair clung to his head and a beard dipped past his waist. He tapped his cane three times against the wooden floor. Instantly the hall became silent. Turning to the giantess and bowing deeply, in that creaky, stuttering way ancient people have of moving, he said, "Princess Gertrude, if it meets your approval, we were just about to begin."

"Yes. Of course, Lester, proceed. Thank you," she replied.

Lester cleared his throat—a process that took a long time considering how old he was and how much buildup he had in his pipes. "Ladies and Lords, thank you for attending the Harvest Ball. As you are aware, our beautiful Princess Gertrude has recently celebrated her three hundredth birthday and has therefore reached marrying age." The crowd clapped politely and Lester continued. "After a careful and extensive search, a groom has been chosen. The Royal Court is delighted to introduce Prince Natas from the Kingdom of Lived and his brother, Ralph."

From out of the shadows, the pair of giants Newton had seen in the forest stepped forward. The taller one, who had been complaining about getting married, bowed and kissed Princess Gertrude's hand. His brother, Ralph, did the same. Newton was shocked. Were these the people they planned to conquer?

The princess graciously accepted the kisses.

"One week from tonight, during the full moon,"

Lester announced, "Gertrude and Natas will marry and our kingdom will once again have a King and Queen." This time the applause was even more enthusiastic.

Prince Natas waited for the crowd to settle before speaking. "I thank you for welcoming my brother and me to your Harvest Ball. Though our people have had problems in the past, I pledge that this marriage will mark a historic beginning. The Merriwarts and Liveds will no longer be enemies, but allies, and together we will live in the greatest kingdom giantkind has ever known! Peace shall once again come to our land. To mark the occasion, as a gift, the Liveds will deliver—" The prince hesitated for dramatic effect as the crowd leaned forward expectantly. "*Water*! More water than if it rained for years. So much that the Merriwarts will never need to worry about it again."

A great roar went up.

Peace! Newton was flabbergasted. Prince Natas was a liar. All he wanted was the Merriwarts' wood. He would kill Gertrude soon after the marriage. These giants believed everything Natas said! The Merriwarts were not only allowing their enemy to marry their princess, but handing them the keys to the kingdom in the process.

So distracted was Newton in thinking about Prince Natas's announcement that he didn't hear the bird's approach or have time to duck out of the way. The bird, which was the same size as Newton, whooshed down, plucked him off the ledge by the scruff of his shirt and had him airborne before he could say, "What the—!"

If you've ever traveled by the beak of a rainbow eagle, you know it is not the most pleasant way to get from A to B. Especially if the bird in question flies so fast as to be almost invisible. Newton felt like he was on a roller coaster that had been set for warp speed. Branches crashed against his legs, leaves slapped his face, the night air flapped against his ears. The bird zigged and zagged, dipped and dove until finally she swerved in through another window and plopped Newton down on a kitchen table.

A giant, with his back to Newton and the bird, was busy chopping vegetables and crying all over the food in a most unhygienic manner. After a couple of minutes, the giant still had not noticed Newton. The bird cawed and the giant turned around.

"Herbert!" Newton shouted when he saw who it was. But Herbert did not seem to share the same enthusiasm for having a reunion with Newton and approached him with the chopping knife still in his hand.

"Herbert! Wait! It's me—Newton! Remember the attic? Herbert, please! What are you doing?"

The giant pushed Newton back on the table and splayed him like a chicken for quartering. He raised the knife. "Making dinner."

"Out of me?" Newton shrieked.

The knife quivered as Herbert hesitated. "I should kill you now and be done with it. Then again, maybe I should tie you up until I figure out a proper recipe—that way you won't lose any of your freshness."

Newton shuddered. Herbert continued. "Humans are a delicacy around these parts. My grandmother makes an excellent Minceman Pie."

"That's disgusting!" Newton said. "I don't believe you."

"Why not?"

"You don't look like the kid-killing kind."

Herbert put the knife down and sighed. "You're right. Actually I'm vegetarian. I don't eat children."

Relieved that his bluff had worked, Newton remembered what Herbert had told him in the attic. "I thought you told me you were king of the giants. What are you doing here in the kitchen working, instead of having fun downstairs at the party?"

"I lied." With that, Herbert collapsed into a chair. He buried his head in his hands and lost it. Full-on waterworks. Newton had never seen a giant cry and he found it was not pretty, especially with a giant as ugly as Herbert. The giant cried so hard and so mournfully that even Newton felt a little teary and crunchy in the back of his throat.

"What's the matter?" he asked gently.

Herbert's lower lip quivered and he inhaled in deep gasps but would not speak.

"Come on," Newton urged, "you can tell me."

"No. You'll laugh."

"I can honestly say I would never laugh at a giant holding a knife."

Herbert wiped his eyes against a grimy sleeve. "Well, okay then." He paused before continuing. "I'm not a leader, I'm a follower. And tonight, Princess Gertrude promised she'd sneak away from the ball and come down here. I made Gargoyle Soup—my specialty. But she never showed up."

"Oh." Newton gulped, remembering what he had heard outside the banquet window. "Do you two . . . go out?"

"She's my sweetheart. We're in love!" he cried. "This was the night I was going to ask her to marry me." From his pocket Herbert took a small package wrapped in leaves, which he opened to reveal a wooden ring. "This is the engagement ring. I made it myself."

Newton was unsure how to proceed. Should he tell Herbert what he knew and risk his wrath or should he remain silent?

"Um, Herbert—" Newton started. "I might have heard wrong, but at the banquet, an old giant named Lester announced that Princess Gertrude would get married in one week to a guy named Prince Natas, who—"

Newton never got a chance to tell Herbert about the forest. "It can't be true!" Herbert broke in. "This is catastrophic! One week! What am I going to do?"

Someone yelled from the room above. "Herbert! Shut your blubbering trap! What's going on down there?"

Instantly Herbert was silent, though a few tears leaked out of his eyes. "Mrs. Hubble!" Steps could be heard up there. "Now I've done it!" Herbert whispered. "She'll be coming down. Once she discovers you"—Herbert held the knife to his neck and made his eyes go buggy—"lights out! Mrs. Hubble likes nothing more than a little Roasted Child." Herbert looked around the room desperately. Mrs. Hubble's steps were growing louder.

"Who's Mrs. Hubble?" Newton asked.

"She's my boss. Chief cook. You don't want to mess with her." Herbert looked around. "Margaret!" he beckoned, and the bird flew over and landed on his arm. Herbert whispered something in her ear.

Just then, Mrs. Hubble entered the room and let out a squeal when she saw Newton. "Oh my! A little boy! We haven't had one of them in eras!" She lunged at Newton with greedy outstretched hands, but before she could pick him up, Margaret plucked Newton off the table and flew out the window.

Mrs. Hubble's cackle chased them into the night. "Darn you, bird! Darn you!"

Newton must have fallen asleep in Margaret's beak, because when he woke the bird was gone and he was back in his attic, his face buried in an old running shoe, and he had a desperate need to use the bathroom. For some unexplained reason his left sock was missing. He had no idea where it could have gone, considering that his shoe was still solidly attached to his foot. It wasn't like it had slipped off or anything.

Newton stuck his head out of the hatch for an exploratory look and saw his four brothers sprawled across his bed, asleep but still dressed. The grays of morning were coming through the window. Newton had been in the attic all night.

Quietly, delicately, Newton rappeled down and picked his way past the bodies, and was almost safely out of the room—when he tripped on a string that had been tied across his bedroom doorway.

Engelbert instantly rolled over and said, "I see our Burmese Mancatcher worked. Get up, prisoner!" Newton stood. His three other brothers were now fully awake. "We have been patient and we have been cunning," Engelbert continued. "This is our reward. Prepare to be punished!"

Terrified of his brothers and more terrified of peeing his pants, Newton did the only sensible thing. He screamed. It was a brilliant tactical move that the quadruplets had not anticipated.

Their father dashed into the bedroom in 2.11 seconds (still displaying some Olympic sprinter speed). "What's going on? Who's hurt?" he said wildly, scanning the room for signs of danger and destruction.

"I must have been having a nightmare," Newton replied innocently.

"And we rushed in to see if our dear brother was okay," Ernest said.

"We were *so* worried," Engelbert added.

His father looked at Newton strangely. "But you're fully dressed."

"Well, thank goodness it was only a dream," Newton said, and hustled off to do his bathroom business before he started peeing out his ears or had to answer any more of his father's questions.

When he was finished washing his hands (scrubbing extra hard in case he had rubbed against a virus), Newton had two options: face his brothers or escape. To create a distraction, Newton turned on the shower, then opened the bathroom window and crawled out into the morning air. He slid down the drainpipe and hurried off to tell Max about his night. Concerned that he had done permanent damage to his digestive system by not eating in such a long time, he hoped that Max's mom had breakfast cooking.

The quadruplets were growing increasingly fidgety in the hallway, waiting outside the bathroom door. After twenty minutes, figuring Newton was about as clean as he was going to get, Earl picked the lock and they stormed the room. At first they couldn't see anything because of the steam, but it didn't take them long to discover Newton's cunning subterfuge. Not only had he once again eluded them, but he had used up all the hot water.

Chapter 4

Mrs. Brown, Max's mom, did not disappoint. When Newton heard the Italian opera blasting out of her kitchen window, he knew the breakfast mother lode would soon be his. Mrs. Brown could not listen to a tenor's *mama mias* without shaking and baking. And how she loved her operas, especially the tragedies.

But Newton waited a few minutes before knocking on the back door, content to watch Mrs. Brown move around the kitchen, feeding Max's baby sister, Wiley, and mixing ingredients. Not for the first time Newton imagined what life might be like as a member of Max's family.

"Newton," Mrs. Brown said when she saw him standing there, "I must not have heard you. Come in." Even though Newton felt entirely too old to be hugged, Mrs. Brown wrapped him in her arms and he was engulfed in warmth and the pleasant smell of baked bread.

No sooner had she released him than a fistful of mush flew past Newton's head, nicking his ear before landing *splat* against the wall. Wiley smiled, scooped out another round of mush and fired again. This time Newton wasn't so lucky and got nailed in the forehead.

"Sorry about that," Mrs. Brown apologized. "Mr. Brown has been teaching her how to throw a curveball."

"He must be a very good teacher, then," Newton replied, wiping the gunk off his forehead.

Mrs. Brown laughed, even though Newton had not intended to make a joke. "You're here awfully early today. Max's not awake yet. Is everything all right, Newton?"

"Fine. Fine. Fine."

"Have you had breakfast?"

"Sort of."

"Either you ate or you didn't," Mrs. Brown insisted.

"Well, if you put it that way, I guess I didn't," Newton admitted.

Mrs. Brown tsk-tsked. "Oh, dear heavens! No wonder you're so gray. Sit down and we'll fix that immediately."

Within minutes Belgian waffles with marshmallow syrup arrived, followed by muffins spread thick with strawberry jam, and then a baloney omelette. The meal was topped off with Newton's most favorite breakfast food of all—a banana split drowning in a river of caramel sauce. It was eating bliss and not once did Newton have to worry about his brothers elbowing and stealing food off his plate, though he made sure to keep an eye on Wiley when Mrs. Brown gave her a bowl of beets.

Max arrived in the kitchen about the time Newton was starting to slump in his seat. "Newton!" he exclaimed when he saw his best friend, "I thought you—"

"—said I'd be here at eight-thirty to walk to school," Newton quickly interjected before Max could squeeze in another word. "But I couldn't sleep and came early instead." Mrs. Brown was busy taking a pineapple upside-down cake out of the oven and had her back to the boys, so Newton slid Max the universal "zip it" symbol. Though Max was obviously puzzled by his friend's secretiveness, he waited until they were outside before asking any questions.

Newton told Max everything, including the part about Prince Natas and his brother. "That's incredible," Max gasped. "We've got to go back and warn them. Strategize about defenses and artillery deployment."

"I'm not so sure," Newton replied. The vision of Mrs. Hubble's attempt to stew him, combined with a lingering fear that he just might have contracted a time bomb of a virus in the Kingdom of the Merriwarts made Newton hesitant—though the anticipation of climbing more of those gigantic trees in daylight was not without its appeal.

"Fate has given us a golden opportunity," Max insisted. "We can't let it slip away."

"An opportunity for what?"

"An opportunity to be *popular*. We'd be heroes if we saved Princess Gertrude's kingdom and we'd be heroes for discovering another world. People will write about our adventures just like they wrote about Christopher Columbus sailing to America or

Neil Armstrong landing on the moon." Max paused before continuing. "Think about it, we'd be the most famous students in the history of Donlands Academy. And let's face it, Newton, for guys like you and me, a chance like that doesn't come around too often. Of course, we'd need documentation."

Secretly Newton always had believed (in spite of his delicate constitution) that he had the right stuff, and Max's idea started taking hold like a fever.

"There's something else too. A long shot, of course, but if we can pull it off, your problems with your psychotic brothers might just be over."

This was beyond belief. Famous was one thing, but life without the quadruplets tormenting him would be miraculous. "How do you figure that?"

"Newton, Newton, Newton," his friend sighed dramatically. "Sometimes you have such a difficult time seeing the forest for the trees. Do I have to spell it out?"

"Y–E–S," Newton replied, annoyed at Max's insistence on being a know-it-all.

"T–B–C," Max said, smiling slyly as the pair approached the schoolyard of Donlands Academy.

"What's T–B–C?" Newton asked.

"To Be Continued. This is no place to discuss strategies. Spies are everywhere. The walls have ears."

"Come on, Max, just tell me."

Max looked at Newton and calmly replied, "Patience. We're way too far behind enemy lines for hasty decisions."

Not for the first time, Newton found himself wishing Max wasn't so easily influenced by his love of espionage, World War II movies, *The Complete Sherlock Holmes Reader* and outdoor survival guides. If there was a hint of camouflage and the possibility of a smoking gun, Max ate it up.

When Newton entered his homeroom, the class went silent. Pencils dropped and chalk stopped squeaking across blackboards. Even Sally Moses (who talked so much people nicknamed her The Auctioneer) halted abruptly on the second syllable of *obnoxious*. Something was definitely wrong and Newton suspected it concerned him. But why? Except for Max, he had no friends. Checking to see if his fly was done up (it was), Newton couldn't imagine why he had everyone's attention. Even his teacher, Mrs. Powell, put down her red attendance pen and seemed to look at Newton in disgust.

As soon as Principal Bell came on the PA for the

daily announcements, Newton understood why. How could he have forgotten?

"I'd like to say on behalf of all the staff and students at Donlands Academy," Principal Bell said, "that Coach Henley will *eventually* be okay. It will take a while, but the doctors say he'll be fine." All eyes were on Newton. Principal Bell continued. "As you probably know, we lost the game. By one goal."

By lunch Newton was a wreck and dared not enter the cafeteria in case someone slipped cyanide into his meat loaf. He was thinking of eating *inside* his locker. Luckily Max had a plan. "I've done some covert work and I've found a safe-house for us." From his vest pocket Max pulled out a key. "The master key that opens every door in the school!"

Newton was in awe. "Where did you get that?"

"A field mission one rainy day in fourth grade. The details will understandably remain sketchy. I need to protect my sources." Max hustled Newton into a janitor's closet. Under threat of enemy attack and amid the strong smell of cleaning detergent, they shared Max's sandwiches knowing the lock was firmly latched.

"Thanks for sticking by me, Max," Newton said. "I was worried you wouldn't be my friend anymore after listening to Bell."

"Like I said last night—before Herbert ate the phone—what you did during the soccer game was an act of cunning—hitting the enemy where it hurts. Never, not for a moment, forget this is war. And in the code of war, what counts most?"

Newton had no idea. "Big tanks?"

"No. It's loyalty. Loyalty counts most. I'll never leave you," Max replied, then added, "Besides, Coach Henley once caught me picking my nose during a baseball game and in front of the whole team told me to stop doing it."

"I remember that."

Max sighed. "Everybody remembers that."

"So tell me about the TBC part of your plan."

"If we can somehow convince Herbert to make a guest appearance in your bedroom, think about the possibilities. He could be your own personal bodyguard. The next time the quadruplets try to hassle you, Herbert sits on them. End of problem."

Newton thought about Max's plan and decided it had its merits. He was in the middle of a pleasant daydream of his brothers squealing under Herbert's weight when the relative peacefulness of the room was shattered by the *screeching* sound of metal on metal. Suddenly smoke and dust filled the air. Newton's eardrums ached and his throat burned.

"We're under fire," Max yelled. "Prepare to defend your territory!"

Max armed himself with a spray-cleaning bottle and tossed another over to Newton. They watched in horror as a whirring blade appeared, cutting a jagged circle into the door. When the piece popped out, Engelbert peered through the new opening. He wasn't even wearing safety goggles.

"Just as I suspected," he said. "Little Newton-poo and his snot-eating friend, Max."

Max let out a spray of cleaning solvent and nailed Engelbert in the eye, forcing him to drop the saw.

Newton fired too, but his bottle was on mist and wasn't nearly as effective. With Engelbert temporarily blinded, they attempted to make a run for it, but Ernest, Earl and Eric were waiting. Ignoring Max, they piled on Newton, scratching, punching and clawing. Max tried every tactic he knew to halt the attack (while continuing to pepper the brothers with cleaning solvent) but nothing worked.

Who knows what might have happened if Principal Bell had not walked by at that moment. Seeing the mass of writhing bodies and flailing limbs, Bell jumped into the fracas and quickly separated Newton from his crazed brothers. At first Newton was so relieved that he wasn't ripped in two he could have hugged Principal Bell. Fortunately he didn't.

"What is the meaning of this!" Bell demanded, looking at Newton and Max.

"We had nothing—" Max began, but Engelbert stepped in, holding up the saw.

"If I may, sir?" Engelbert asked. Tears were still running down his face from the solvent. By this point a decent-size mob of kids had gathered.

"Of course," Principal Bell replied.

"As much as it pains me to rat on my own brother, in this case, I feel I have no choice. I caught Newton and Max sawing a hole in the janitor's closet. When we tried to stop them, they fought back. Especially Newton."

The students gasped. A bead of sweat formed on the principal's forehead and his face went a Merry Christmas shade of red. "Is this true?" he spat out, grinding his molars so hard that dental surgery would be required to repair the enamel.

"No!" Newton exclaimed. "I haven't even taken woodworking class yet."

"Absolutely not!" Max replied.

Engelbert turned to Bell and shook his head sadly. "The boy who sent Coach Henley to the hospital is calling me a liar. How utterly pathetic . . . sir."

When you consider how horrific Newton's day had been, getting suspended for the rest of the week wasn't exactly punishment. He hoped that by the time they allowed him back in school, kids would have again forgotten who he was.

Max was positively buoyant about also getting the rest of the week off school. "Don't you see, Newton, it couldn't have worked out any better if we had planned it. After a brief field meeting at HQ for a debriefing and supplies, we'll be on our way."

The field meeting between Max and his mother was surprisingly short. He told her what happened, and Mrs. Brown believed him. As simple as that. No questions, no accusations, no yelling—nothing except, "Well, that man needs to get his head examined. I always suspected Principal Bell of being a top-drawer fascist."

Newton had no idea what a fascist was, but he knew, when his parents got home, it would be an entirely different conversation. The quadruplets would see to that. Newton could not remember the last time his parents took his side. On anything. The only positive thing he could think of was that they both worked until dinner.

Newton and Max sat in the Wigginses' attic. Newton, who hadn't slept much in the past day and a half, was tired. His eyelids screamed and his head buzzed. "I don't know, Max," Newton argued. "Maybe we should wait. I'm not so sure I'm ready to go back just yet."

Max unscrewed the cap of his canteen and took a long sip of grape juice, then recapped. "Don't tell me you're scared."

"I'm not scared. It's just—"

"Just what? Would you feel safer wearing the helmet?" Max asked, holding out his authentic, army issue, camouflage headgear. There was a bullet hole right through the front. After Max first bought it, he spent hours unsuccessfully trying to find flecks of dried blood and brains. Newton figured someone just drilled a hole through the metal to jack up the price, but he never told Max.

He handed Newton the canteen. "Soldier, I'm worried about dehydration. Drink." Newton took a swig and indeed felt slightly less woozy. "Let's move this operation out," Max ordered, and they began to crawl (at Max's insistence) along the attic floor, toward the small red door.

As they approached, the smell of something dead grew stronger. The odor was awful. Max gagged (mostly for effect) and Newton concentrated on taking shallow breaths.

"I think we're under gas attack. I should have brought the masks. My lungs are melting," Max declared dramatically.

Newton braved ahead and soon discovered the

source of the noxious fumes: a dead mouse with a thumbtack through its tail was pinned to the door.

"Holy smokes!" Max said. "Where'd that come from?"

Newton had no idea. The mouse, though slightly shriveled and definitely dead, seemed to be staring at them.

"What should we do?" Max asked. "I mean, this is sinister. Do you think your brothers aced the rodent?"

"Maybe. I wouldn't put cruelty to animals past them. I wonder why, though."

They stared at the mouse corpse for a couple of minutes, unsure of how best to carry out removal procedures. Max suggested it would be good training for Newton to do the actual removing. Newton used an old work shirt and delicately pried off the critter, hoping he wasn't exposing himself to undue cootie contamination.

As soon as the mouse had been done away with, Max found himself restored to his usual brave self. He handed Newton the flashlight. "I'll take it from here," he commanded. "Cover me. Watch my back." However, when Max tried to turn the handle of the door nothing happened. It wouldn't budge.

"What's wrong?" Newton asked.

"It doesn't seem to want to open. How'd you do it?"

"I just turned. That's all. Here, let me try." Newton pulled and pried, he jiggled and he squeezed, but he couldn't budge the door either. In spite of throwing everything they had into it, the boys were stumped. The door would not open.

"Maybe it's been hexed," Max suggested. "Suppose someone discovered how you snuck in and hexed it shut again. Did you ever wonder what Herbert was looking for when you first saw him?"

"I remember him saying something about wanting to go into my attic."

"That's incredible! Why?"

"I don't know. He was about to tell me when Margaret the bird appeared, and he took off before I got an answer."

"An evil prince, hexed doors, a love-struck giant and a beautiful princess. This has *conspiracy* written all over it. We've got to somehow figure out a way to get back in there. We'll need some professional help."

Without any other options, the boys climbed out of the attic and lay on Newton's bedroom floor, staring at the ceiling, trying to figure out their next move. After four minutes Newton sat up and declared, "I've got it! Witch Hazel. If there is anyone who can help us out, it's her. She's supposed to know all about this kind of stuff."

Raising an eyebrow suspiciously, Max looked at Newton and gulped. "You are aware of her reputation as a child-eating witch?"

"Rumors. Name one kid that you know she's actually eaten."

"Come on, Newton, there has to be somewhere else we can turn, someone else we can talk to. No one has ever gone in there and made it out alive. Remember what happened to Frank Baptiste the Halloween he egged her house?"

Newton remembered. How could he forget? Frank and the quadruplets were friends. Nobody could say for sure exactly what happened—all Newton knew was that Frank set off alone to egg Witch Hazel's house. The next time he was seen, he couldn't talk without stuttering and his eyes twitched constantly, like he was trying to blink out specks of dust. Most horribly of all, his Halloween candy had vanished, never to be seen again.

Frank had not been the same since and refused to talk about it.

Ignoring Max's dire warning, Newton pulled out the phone book and looked up Witch Hazel's number. Nervously he dialed. The phone rang. And rang. And rang. Newton was about to hang up when an ancient, cackling voice answered.

"Hello, Newton Wiggins."

He couldn't believe it. "How do you know it's me?"

"Come to my house at midnight. Knock three times first. If you want information." As abruptly as the conversation started, it ended.

Witch Hazel had hung up!

Newton put the receiver down.

"What? What'd she say? You okay, Newton? You don't look so hot."

Shaking, Newton took the blanket from his bed and wrapped it around himself. "Maybe you're right. Witch Hazel is a bad idea."

"What did she say? What did she say?" Max asked excitedly.

Newton told Max the entire conversation, word for word.

"Way too much risk. It's settled then, we don't go. This ends right here," Max declared. "It's over."

"I guess it is," Newton agreed, and shivered again. His eyes watered, a sure sign that an illness was about to descend. He hoped that this time it would be full-blown pneumonia and he would miss even more school.

Secretly Newton was relieved that Max hadn't wanted to visit Witch Hazel. Twelve o'clock was definitely too late to be out on a school night (suspension or no suspension). He was also glad the door was shut tight. He was tired and had had enough adventure for a while.

Just then, they heard the front door open. "Uh-oh," Newton said. "My parents are home. You might want to climb out the bathroom window. This could get ugly."

"Yeah, I think I will. Good luck. Call me later . . . if you can." And Max put on his combat helmet and left.

Newton huddled in the blanket and pretended to be asleep.

Chapter 5

His mother and father entered the room.

"Newton, are you awake?" his father asked.

"I think I may be sick," Newton offered lamely.

His mother felt his forehead. "It doesn't feel hot."

"Sick or not sick, we've got a problem," his father announced. "Get up."

Newton hopped out of bed.

"Young man," his mother said, "do you have any idea who we received a call from today?"

"Help us understand," his father added.

Newton's knees shook and he was trying his best not to cry. "It wasn't my fault."

"We know exactly what happened. Engelbert told us everything," his mother explained.

"But, I—"

"You've let yourself down," his father stated. "That's the worst part."

His parents stared at Newton as he shuffled his feet. His legs were lead. His eyes stung so he wiped them with his sleeve.

"Well . . . ?" his mother asked impatiently.

"Well . . . what?" Newton replied hesitantly, unsure of how he was supposed to answer the question.

"Do you have anything else to say for yourself?" his father asked.

Newton hesitated and then sighed. "No," he replied flatly, knowing explaining was useless. The quadruplets had strength in numbers. By himself, without hard evidence, he would never convince his parents to believe his side of the story.

"I didn't think so," his father said. "As much as I hate to do this, you're grounded." He took a deep breath and counted to ten before proceeding, this time more slowly. "Tonight, in celebration of the quadruplets scoring twenty-two goals—*against* the other team—at their soccer game, your mother is making tuna casserole. Unfortunately you won't be joining us."

His mother patted his head. "And unfortunately you won't be going to the baseball game with us tomorrow either."

"We have front-row seats. You would have loved it," his father added, not altogether unkindly.

Newton wouldn't have wanted to go even if they were sitting on the pitching mound.

After his parents left, Newton just stared at the wall—not blinking, not focusing, not moving, not thinking, not feeling—simply trying to remain as still as he could. But that didn't last long and even though he was ten, tears fell, chasing each other in quick succession.

This was an all-time low. He had never disappointed his parents so much for doing nothing. They weren't even mad. That was the worst part. More times than he could count, Newton had been grounded or missed dinner because of some deviousness the quadruplets had framed him for. But somehow this felt different.

It was at moments like this that Newton was convinced he must have been adopted, or switched at birth in the hospital nursery ward. The quadruplets were always right. They were perfect and he was a criminal.

But soon the crying ran its course. After eating two chocolate bars from the stash he kept hidden for just such emergencies, Newton felt slightly better. With an evening of solitary confinement in front of him, he decided to make the best use of his time and took down the dictionary from his shelf. Inside, Newton had used an Exacto knife to hollow out a space to hide his current journal. He knew his brothers would never open a dictionary—too many words and not enough pictures for them.

Journal #22 was a loose-leaf notebook that Newton had been working on for the past three months. Journals #1 to #21 of the series were stashed in a trunk in the attic. They were notebooks he had been writing all his ideas in since he was five. In them were the innovations and inspirations of a scientific nature that were always spilling out of Newton's head. The journals contained everything from sketches of space suits that could withstand Saturn's atmospheric conditions to schematic diagrams and equations for a time machine. Newton had never told anyone about the journals because the first rule of inventing, as everybody knows, is never tell anyone what you're inventing. When he won the Nobel Prize for science, Newton would show the world his journals, explaining how they laid the foundation for all that came later.

Journal #22 contained information on Newton's latest invention: a pair of fully functioning wings.

The wings were a stroke of genius that had consumed Newton since the summer. Of considerable help was Professor A. E. Wilson's book *Theoretic Flight: A User's Manual*, which Newton had all but memorized.

Once the schematic diagrams were finished, he began secretly building the prototype—custom-fitted to his anatomical specifications. Newton patched together the wings from old kites retrieved on tree-climbing expeditions. What he lacked in sewing skill, Newton more than made up for by reinforcing all of the seams with fishing line and glue. Using his family's tent poles, Newton soldered together a frame for the wings. He hoped that by the time they needed the tent for another camping trip, Newton's invention would already be making money and he could afford to replace the parts he had destroyed.

The big *eureka!* moment came when Newton finally figured out a way around the fact he would never have the strength to generate enough FPMS (flaps per minute). He rigged up a series of pulleys and rejigged a small battery-powered engine to provide power. The result: a contraption that might just fly. It was difficult to keep a project like this secret, but Newton stored the wings under the mattress and only worked on his invention long after his family had gone to sleep. No one knew about it. Not even Max.

Newton dared not take the wings out in case someone came in the room, but as he reviewed his notes he felt a flush of excitement. If (and of course this was a big if) his calculations were correct, there was no reason why he wouldn't be the first boy to realize self-propelled flight. All he needed was an opportunity to field-test the machine.

Newton heard footsteps and quickly shut Journal #22, hiding it under a pile of comics. His brothers barged in the room eating Eskimo Pies, their faces smeared with ice cream and chocolate.

"Shake our hands," Earl ordered, sticking out a

sticky paw. "Congratulate us on our soccer game. We won twenty-two–nothing, and Engelbert scored seven goals and the rest of us got four each. No one else on the team scored, not even once."

"That doesn't add up. Four plus four plus four plus seven equals nineteen, not twenty-two," Newton replied.

"It does too, moron," said Earl. "Now, shake our hands."

Not wanting to get into an arithmetic debate with a group so notoriously bad at math that they could never be It in hide-and-seek because of counting limitations, Newton dropped the matter and reluctantly started shaking, weakly offering congratulations on their soccer exploits. Each brother gripped as tightly as he could, so that by the time Newton got to Engelbert, his knuckles were blue and his hand was numb.

Engelbert stared at Newton and said, "This is for scoring on your own net. We're still not even for that yet." Engelbert locked both his hands around Newton's and began administering the famous Chinese Death Grip. Of course, Newton had read about the Grip, had heard kids in the schoolyard talking about this torture method in hushed awe, but until now he had believed it was only a myth.

His knees went weak and he felt he might faint. Engelbert continued his relentless squeezing.

"Say 'congratulations'!"

At that moment, there was nothing in the world Newton felt like doing more. But he couldn't speak. The grip had a stranglehold on his vocal cords. The pressure could have made a stone weep.

"*Say* it!" Engelbert urged.

And still, Newton could not even mutter a moan.

Thankfully, he barfed, which forced Engelbert to release his hand and deal with the mess that had landed, bull's-eye, all over him.

"Congratulations on scoring seven goals. I know you won't believe me, but I'm sorry about puking on your clothes," Newton weakly offered, then scrammed to wash his face and brush his teeth.

When Newton returned from the bathroom, the quadruplets were gone. Though his hand ached—it was somewhat bruised—Newton didn't think any bones were broken. After cleaning up his mess and opening his windows to air out the room, Newton decided to look over Journal #22 one final time before bed—that way his unconscious would have all night to allow any new ideas a chance to brew (a common trick all the great inventors used).

He lifted up the comic books, but #22 was gone!

Impossible! Newton was positive that he had hidden it before the quadruplets—

Frantically, desperately, he searched behind the desk, through drawers, under piles of books, everywhere, on the slim chance that the journal had been mislaid.

Then he saw their sign. Tacked to the closet door was a piece of paper that read, GUESS WHAT WE HAVE, PUKE BOY? NOW WE'RE EVEN! HA! HA! HA! HA!

The quadruplets had stolen his journal! Of all the low-down, barrel-scraping, maggot-eating, sneaky things they had ever done to him, this was rock bottom.

Newton was absolutely furious. His ears burned, his legs twitched and his stomach did jumping jacks in anger. Never in his life had he felt such rage. *How could they!*

He was all set to storm their room and demand his journal back, no matter what the consequences, when it hit him: He'd lose. His brothers would lie and his parents would believe them. No matter how right Newton was, the quadruplets would win. In all likelihood, for causing the commotion, he would be handed a double-life grounding sentence and Newton wouldn't see sunshine again until he turned sixty-five. And, of course, they'd still have the journal.

Newton stomped back and forth across his room, trying to figure out a plan of attack. Crying was pointless (besides, it felt like he had produced a river of tears in the past day alone). Justice was a joke. The more he paced, the angrier he became. Finally his father banged a broom on the ceiling below and yelled, "Keep it down! You're supposed to be grounded!" and Newton flopped on his bed, but not before frustratedly kicking a big dent in his Dallas Cowboys wastepaper basket, a birthday present his parents had surprised him with last year and been so proud to give him.

Admitting the journal was all but lost forever (he imagined his brothers had probably set it on fire or passed it through their mother's paper shredder by now), Newton continued to stew. His options were limited. Every revenge scenario he devised could be easily quashed. But by stealing the journal, the quadruplets had crossed a line. As sure as dogs will turn white snow yellow, Newton realized the years he had spent hoping, waiting, expecting the glorious day to arrive when his brothers would leave him alone was a foolish dream. They would never stop tormenting him. And he was sick of the abuse, fed up with a lifetime of unsuccessfully staying out of their way.

Then, like a flash, it came to him—Max was right! Newton understood what he had to do. The only language bullies spoke fluently was intimidation, and Newton knew Herbert—with the proper guidance—could intimidate the hubcaps off a race car.

If somehow Newton could get Herbert into his attic . . . the next time the quadruplets came barging into his room, they would meet his very own, personal bodyguard. The vision of Herbert bullying the bullies made Newton entirely forget he had been feeling sorry for himself.

He would visit Witch Hazel.

Chapter 6

Newton waited until he was absolutely sure everyone was asleep before setting out on his mission. The house was silent except for the low rumble of snoring. Still, Newton knew his brothers had most likely set up another Burmese Mancatcher or some other even more ingenious trap to catch him as soon as he stepped into the hallway. Instead he would have to attempt to exit the house by another more daring route—out his bedroom window!

His window was twenty feet off the ground and even for a master climber like Newton it presented a challenge—there was nothing on the side of the house to grab hold of.

But Newton was not planning to climb; he was going to fly out the window!

And no time like the present to test his invention. After nervously lifting up the mattress and sliding out the wings, Newton stuffed a basketball and some bunched-up clothes under his sheets to make it look like he was still sleeping. To protect himself against the night air, Newton wore a blue wool sweater.

The engine and batteries for his invention were stored in an old army knapsack that Max had given him for his eighth birthday. Newton lay the wings on the floor and put the knapsack between them. Then, taking a spool of rope he had bought at the hardware store, Newton began the process of rigging the device together, forcing himself to go slowly to avoid making any mistakes. His hands were shaking with excitement as he looped the rope through grommets and pulleys and cinched knots tightly.

Twice he peered out his bedroom door to see if anyone had stirred.

They hadn't.

When the rigging was complete Newton lay on the floor, slid on the knapsack and awkwardly strapped on the wings. The process would have gone much more easily with an assistant but eventually Newton managed to hook everything up.

Though his room was cramped, Newton had just enough space to take a few test flaps and ensure a rope wouldn't get jammed or a pulley tangled. He had to be careful not to crash a delicate wing against a wall. As soon as he raised his arms, the battery kicked in, the pulleys glided smoothly, and he started silently lifting off the ground. Newton couldn't believe it! Flapping was effortless. The wings felt like they had always been a part of him. Bird-boy was airborne (even if it was only a couple of inches off the ground). Not daring to risk possible damage in such a confined space or bash his head on the ceiling, Newton stopped and made his way toward the window.

The moment of truth had arrived. What better way to find out whether or not his invention would work than by hurling himself out the second-floor window? After all, when Edison plugged in his first lightbulb he risked electrocution, and when Henry Ford backed his beloved Model T out of the garage, there was the distinct possibility the brakes wouldn't work or the steering would fail and he'd end up crashing into the side of a barn.

Newton angled himself out the window.

Perched on the ledge outside his bedroom window, staring at the driveway below, Newton began doubting the decision to conduct his maiden flight so high off the ground. It was one thing to draw schematic diagrams and build a model, it was another thing altogether to hope (and perhaps pray) that all his calculations were correct, that the invention wouldn't tear apart, that a thousand things that could go wrong, wouldn't. The night was cold and his breath was visible and Newton was having second, third, fourth and fifth thoughts about this enterprise.

Twice he bent his knees and willed himself to push off, and twice he chickened out. His hands and ears were starting to get cold. *Come on, Wiggins. It's only gravity*, he told himself, hoping to kick-start some courage, but still he stubbornly clung to the window ledge.

Who knows, if left to his own devices, whether Newton eventually would have jumped. But when lights went on in his bedroom and Newton turned and saw his father standing at the door, that was the only push Newton needed.

Without thinking he leaped into the night. And then Newton was falling, plunging toward the driveway with alarming speed. He had completely forgotten to review his flight plan checklist. With his eyes shut and his limbs refusing to listen to his brain—which kept shouting, *"Flap! Flap! Flap!"*—he was in deep trouble. At the last moment, mere inches from certain death (or at least making a big dent in the driveway), he finally remembered to open his wings . . . and a pocket of air lifted him upward.

Immediately Newton started flapping and, to his great relief, began to rise. At first slowly because he only took little flaps. But as he gained confidence and got the feel of the machine, soon he went higher and higher—past houses, past telephone wires, past trees, until there was nothing but sky between himself and the stars. Though the cold air made his eyes sting (next time he would bring his aviator goggles), Newton Wiggins was thrilled.

He'd had done it! His invention worked! And flying was everything he had hoped! By dipping an arm Newton could turn and spiral in circles; to go higher he simply tilted the wings back and flapped. He soared in and out of air pockets, dipsy-doodling in the night sky, exhilarated to race the moon.

At first it was difficult to tell exactly where he was, but soon landmarks became recognizable,

even if they looked completely different from so high up. He debated whether to stop at Max's to ask if he wanted to rendezvous at Witch Hazel's, but it was already well past midnight and Newton was worried that if he arrived too late, Witch Hazel might turn him into a toad.

As he soared over the Donlands Academy track, over the Lyles' pool, over the Kerwin Shopping Mall, over the railroad tracks, Newton felt happy. Not just a glad-to-be-alive kind of happiness, but a pure, inexpressible joy that ran from his toes to the top of his head. This was a glee unlike anything Newton had ever experienced. For the first time in as long as he could recall, he felt competent, useful, coordinated—all of the qualities the quadruplets kept insisting he was born without. It was great to be an inventor. No one else (that he knew of) owned a pair of working wings, and Newton was pretty certain he was the only boy in his town out flying around that night.

Even from the air, Witch Hazel's house loomed large. Two towers rose up to meet the night. Legend had it that the house had belonged to Witch Hazel's parents before they both died in a terrible car crash when she was still a little girl. No one dared to try to rescue the orphaned little girl because, even back then, the house was supposed to be haunted. Miraculously, the girl survived, grew up and eventually became an old hag. How she had managed to find food and clothing was anyone's guess but there were the usual suspicions about deals with the devil and selling of souls. Of course, nothing was ever confirmed.

As he flew closer, Newton wished the meeting

were taking place during daylight. Why did witches keep such ghoulish hours? The house was ominously dark; not a single light was on. He thought he could make out tombstones in the backyard, poking above the uncut grass. Shutters flapped in the wind, trees creaked, frogs ribitted.

Slowly Newton began his descent, circling the house, looking for a place to land, but as he came closer, a black cloud kept blocking his path. No matter which direction Newton turned, the cloud appeared to move toward him. Newton was confused. What was it? Smoke? A storm cloud? Nerve gas? As it came ever closer, the black mass seemed almost alive. Panicked, with his arms starting to tire from the flying, Newton was desperate to land, yet he had no idea whether he was eight inches or eighty feet off the ground.

Newton almost fainted when he realized what was about to engulf him—bats! But by that time it was too late to swerve.

Hundreds, maybe thousands, of furry creatures flapping their moist wings came at Newton. A swarm of tiny claws clamped onto Newton's clothes and skin, struggling to maintain their grip. Newton couldn't move, couldn't see, could barely breathe and, most terrifying of all, couldn't hear.

Within moments, not an inch of him was left unexposed. Bodies upon bodies pressed in, blocking out all noise. Newton imagined that this must be what it felt like to drown and he tried not to think about suffocating. He closed his eyes. Bat wings tickled his nose.

Newton had no idea how long he was held in their grip.

When the bats finally released Newton and flew away, he was shocked to discover that

1. he wasn't dead.
2. he had landed in Witch Hazel's front yard.

Aside from the lingering suspicion that he had been exposed to a wicked case of the cooties, Newton was fine. There wasn't a bite, a scratch or even one bat dropping on him. He removed the wings, took off the knapsack and cautiously walked up to the porch.

The front door was open. A serious security risk.

"Hello?" Newton whispered. No one answered and it took everything he had to remain on the porch and not run for dear life. He tried calling again, this time a little louder. Still no one answered. He croaked louder still and started counting—one Mississippi, two Mississippi . . .—deciding that if no one answered by ten, he would fly home.

At eight, a voice cackled out of what Newton had thought was a hole beside the door but quickly realized was the mouth of a python.

"Who's there?"

Newton jumped back. "It's me, Newton Wiggins."

"The boy. Of course. Are you alone?"

"Yes."

"Then, enter . . . ," the voice ominously added, *". . . if you dare."* Newton thought he heard laughter, but could not be certain. The snake had closed its mouth.

Ducking under a cobweb of prehistoric-spider proportions, Newton stepped through the front door. The house was dark and smelled like rotten eggs and wet leaves. Had something died? Was Witch Hazel a murderer? Newton wished he had written his will before he left home (to make sure Max inherited all his notebooks).

Newton crept deeper and deeper into the house, feeling along the walls, hoping to find a light switch. In the dark he couldn't go more than a couple of feet before bumping into something horrifyingly strange—coffins, bones, mummies? These unidentifiable objects made him shudder and he sensed evil spirits hovering uncomfortably close.

The wind picked up and tree branches screeched against the house, like fingernails against a blackboard.

It got worse when Newton mistakenly stepped on a cat. The offended animal let out such a loud *meowww!* Newton was sure he had pulled a heart muscle.

"Marmalade!" Witch Hazel yelled. "My precious, what has he done to you?"

"Sorry. Sorry. I'm s-sorry," Newton stuttered. "I can't see. I think I stepped on a cat. Do you have any lights? It would help."

"You're getting closer. Come down to the basement," the witch ordered. "Hurry up. The brew is almost ready."

Newton would have given anything to be back safely in his room. Haunted houses were infinitely worse than his brothers' cruelest torture. But since he had no idea where the front door was, his only option was to keep walking, arms outstretched in a bad imitation of Frankenstein.

Finally he found, or rather felt, the stairs to the basement. As he went down, with each step, Newton was convinced something or someone was waiting, ready to slice his head off. A mysterious creature (perhaps another python) slithered around his feet and brushed against his ankles. Still he descended. Step after step after step. The stone walls were moist and clammy and the air grew colder, damper.

"Hello?" he called again, his voice hollow, his tongue dry, his throat tight. There was no reply.

Newton felt as if he had gone halfway down to China by the time he saw a faint light ahead. He followed it. When he turned a corner, Witch Hazel was there, stirring a black, boiling cauldron and chanting.

She stopped and turned when Newton appeared. Her face was shriveled and her hands shook. She was the oldest person Newton had ever seen.

"You're late."

"Sorry. I had some delays," Newton apologized.

"I was worried. I even sent my bats out looking for you." The witch locked eyes with Newton and he could not turn away. Her green eyes glowed and bore into him so intently that he felt exposed, like she could see inside—intestines and everything. "You're a brave boy," Witch Hazel croaked, then added, "but perhaps foolish. We shall soon discover which."

The hairs on the back of Newton's neck danced. "To be honest, I don't feel so brave. In fact, I'm really scared right now. This place gives me the creeps."

"Thank you. It took me years of neglect to achieve the effect. That's the nicest thing anyone's said to me in a long while. Actually, come to think of it, it's the only thing anyone's said to me. Haven't had any visitors in the past few decades."

Witch Hazel started stirring again. "I'm almost done. This will help you get back to where you want to go."

Newton was surprised Witch Hazel knew about getting back to the Kingdom of the Merriwarts.

"You might want to stand back," she warned. "Sometimes things get a little . . . um . . . well . . . explosive when I cook."

Newton stood against the wall and watched as Witch Hazel rummaged through drawers, pulling out dried frogs, vulture feathers and other objects that Newton could not identify. She stirred and she sniffed, she churned, chopped and chanted, ignoring Newton, concentrating on her elixir.

> Newt's fingers and grasshopper toes,
> Into the pot, it all goes.
> A dash of ogre and a pinch of dragon spice.
> Don't forget to add four dozen barbecued mice.

The potion is strong, but still not complete,
How tasteless it would be without leprechauns' feet.
Let it simmer, let it boil, let it curdle and cook.
Now toss in the dragon hair stolen by the crook.
Almost done, but there's one thing I forgot—
Oh yes, of course, a piece of witch's snot.

With that, Witch Hazel fished around her left nostril and dug out the biggest booger Newton had ever seen. She expertly flicked it into the pot, stirred a couple more times and ladled out a scoopful. Passing the steamy liquid under her nose, she then delicately sniffed. "A little on the tart side, but I think it will be potent enough for our purposes. This should be enough to put a little more fizz in your imagination."

Witch Hazel handed the ladle to Newton.

"You expect me to drink that?" Newton asked, his gag reflex fluttering at the back of his throat. "Can't you just put a hex on me or something?"

Witch Hazel laughed, her chuckles making the whiskers on the tip of her chin twitch. "You're funny. If you hope to go back to the land of the

Merriwarts, you'll drink this before it gets cold. Make sure you get every last drop down."

"But what happens if I get sick?"

"Well, usually you see a doctor. Why?"

"No. I mean, what happens if I get sick from drinking the brew?"

Witch Hazel paused to consider the question. "Well, I suppose your skin could erupt in boils, your hair could melt, your tongue could swell to two hundred times its normal size or, if I've really botched this up, you could die. Other than that, you should be fine."

Newton gulped. "Die?"

"Don't be so negative. If this does indeed kill you, I promise it will be quick and painless. You won't feel a thing. Honest."

Because Newton had always imagined that he would die some slow and torturous death, quick and painless did not seem that bad. So he pinched his nose and drank. The sorcerer's soup burned his mouth and throat, but he dared not stop and sip for fear of gagging. Newton felt certain he was going to throw up, but he didn't and managed to swallow every last bit.

Witch Hazel smiled. "Enchanted broomsticks! I can't believe you just did that."

"Neither can I, to tell you the truth."

"How was it?"

"A little on the gross side."

Witch Hazel blushed. "That's so kind of you to say. Ogre Brew is one of my specialties. Would you like some more?"

"Will it help?"

"No. Won't make a bit of difference. That should be more than enough to top up your imagination."

Newton was confused. "Top up my imagination? What do you mean?"

"I'll explain later. Come on. We're off to the attic to find out if I'm half the witch I think I am."

Upstairs the wind had worked itself into an even greater rage. As soon as Hazel hobbled into a room, candles magically lit themselves, flickering and sending eerie shadows dancing against the stained walls. Surprisingly, Newton wasn't nearly as frightened as he had been earlier. Hazel continued up the steps and Newton followed.

Outside the attic door, Hazel put her finger to her lips and whispered, "Don't make any quick movements, they won't like that." Before Newton had a chance to ask who "they" were, she opened the door to reveal a room with hundreds of bats hanging from the rafters. Newton thought he recognized one or two of them. New arrivals constantly swooped in through a small pipe in the roof, found a perch, folded up their wings and rested.

Newton found the room oddly peaceful—as long as he didn't think too much about the bats.

Hazel hobbled over to the window and pulled back the thick velvet drapes. She shivered with excitement. "This is going to be more fun than playing with slugs! Come here, Newton. I want you to tell me what you see."

He peered out the window, expecting nearly deserted streets—perhaps Mr. Evans, the town insomniac, or maybe a family of raccoons waddling back from a successful garbage raid. Instead the street was alive with activity. Well, not exactly alive in the flesh-and-blood sense of the word but rather alive with spirits, ghosts, elves, goblins, leprechauns and all manner of UFAs (Unidentifiable Flying Apparitions), busily hovering, floating and passing through their surroundings and each other (except for the leprechauns and elves, who had more substance to them and required considerably more squeezing effort).

Newton blinked. Swallowed. Blinked again and

shook his head. Still, the street was teeming with creatures. Newton was worried his brain was having some kind of seizure.

After a few more moments of staring Newton said, "I don't mean to be rude, but what the heck is going on?" He only said "heck" because he was more than a little uneasy and felt a medium-strength cuss word might settle him down. It didn't.

Witch Hazel put her hands to her mouth and smiled. "Bat's breath! The potion worked!"

In fact, the potion had worked spectacularly in topping up Newton's imagination to full strength. Witch Hazel explained that what Newton was seeing were creatures who inhabited the curious world of Half Life. They weren't fully alive, nor were they dead.

Newton had no idea what Witch Hazel was talking about.

She continued from another angle. "Do you remember when you were younger and talked to your stuffed animals? Played with friends that only you could see? Saw monsters in dark corners? Waited for the tooth fairy to come? Hoped to find an elf?"

Newton told Hazel about his teddy bear Mugsy.

The stuffed animal was Newton's number one best friend until the tragic day his brothers stole him and burned him in the barbecue pit. By the time Newton discovered the theft, Mugsy had been reduced to ashes.

"Personally I've always hated teddy bears. Ogres are much more to my liking." Hazel paused. "Where was I? Oh yes, at the time, did you think Mugsy was real?"

"Sure, but that was just my imagination."

No sooner had Newton said this than Witch Hazel clamped a hand across his mouth. "Don't even think that. The potion will wear off." Then she went on to explain all about the imagination—how as children grow older, they are trained to see less and less of this imaginary world. Adults tell them, "Oh dear, don't be ridiculous, there's not a green monster under your bed" or raise an eyebrow and suspiciously ask, "Who are you talking to?" Soon children question their imaginations (which is the absolute worst thing for an imagination, as it's the most fragile part of the brain). Without constant nurturing, encouragement and support, the imagination withers away until all that's left is reality.

At that point Witch Hazel spat on the ground in

disgust. "Reality! What in the name of flying unicorns is the good of reality? Reality is so— Now what's the word I'm looking for?" She paused and scratched her chin before shouting, "**Boring!**"

The bats fluttered but didn't swarm.

She continued. "Who knows when it began? All that is certain is that eventually almost everyone over the age of eleven had their imaginations wiped out. My Ogre Brew simply restored yours. At full strength, you'll be able to read a portal map."

"How come you never lost your imagination?" Newton asked.

"I was abandoned after my parents died. Best thing that could have happened, really. Though I was a little lonely at the time. You see, there was no one around to try to convince me that what I saw wasn't real, so I never stopped believing."

"Because I drank the potion, I'm now able to see again?"

"Sort of. Fortunately most of your imagination hadn't been destroyed. I'm curious, are you an obedient boy?"

Newton hesitated. "They say I don't follow instructions very well. I'm always getting in trouble for doing things I'm not supposed to. I don't know why, I can't seem to help it."

"Just as I suspected. Admirable traits in a young boy. It's such a pity that there are far too many obedient children roaming around who insist on believing everything they hear. With no imaginations, how dull their lives must be."

At that moment, Marmalade, the cat Newton had stepped on earlier, walked into the room, carrying a roll of parchment between its teeth. Marmalade took one look at Newton, dropped the parchment and hissed.

"Marmalade! Manners, please! We have a guest!" Hazel ordered. She turned to Newton. "I'm so sorry. Marmalade just hasn't been herself since we got back from the annual Witches Convention. I'm worried one of my colleagues hexed her."

"I think it's because I stepped on her earlier," Newton admitted.

"Even so, I'm convinced she's hexed."

Hazel picked up the parchment and handed it to Newton.

Newton unrolled it. At first glance it appeared to be a regular street map of the town, but on closer examination, doors and tunnels rose from the paper. A red circle had been drawn around home plate at the Owls Baseball Stadium.

"I don't understand—what is this?"

"A standard-issue map of apparitions and portals that will access other worlds. Extremely useful in locating alternative realities." Hazel pointed to the red circle. "To avoid confusion—I'd never forgive myself if you ended up in the Land of Nasty Nasty—I circled the portal that will allow you back into the Kingdom of the Merriwarts. If I remember correctly from my last trip there, it's a fairly straightforward route. Keep in mind, however, that the portals are only open at certain times. The one you want will be open for exactly thirty-three seconds starting at four this afternoon."

Hazel looked out the window again. The moon was low in the sky. She yawned. "Morning is almost here—that means it's time for this old bag of bones to get some ugly-rest."

"Thanks for everything," Newton said.

"Don't mention it. Come back again and I'll make you a proper meal. I do a Frog Liver Stew that's out of this world. Seriously. It's made with dead-vampire limbs." Hazel was about to leave the room when she remembered something. "I almost forgot. Whatever else, don't let anyone older than eleven see the map—the consequences would be disastrous. Once a person's imagination reaches a certain point of decay, looking at a map like this could blow their mind. Possibly brains all over the place. It could be a mess."

With that, her magic broom shot into the room, missing Newton by inches. Hazel mounted the broom, tipped her hat and said, "My knees can't take walking down the stairs. Good luck!" Hazel rocketed down out of the room and into the hallway with alarming speed for such an ancient sorcerer. Newton wondered if she got in many accidents.

Newton carefully folded the map and tucked it in his pocket, put on his wings and flew out the window. His second takeoff was much more successful than his first. As he soared over the town, Newton observed spirits and UFAS scurrying about, trying to get some last-minute haunting in before dawn; leprechauns carrying pots of gold; and monsters exiting houses after a night spent making strange noises.

The sun was just starting to crawl over the horizon when Newton landed on his windowsill (a rather difficult flying maneuver that required him to do an impressive reverse hover). Aside from a perplexed family of squirrels in the oak tree, Newton thought no one noticed a flying boy entering 228 Bessborough Drive through the second-floor bedroom window.

He was wrong. But he would find out about that later.

After hiding his wings, Newton lay on his bed. He made a mental list of all the things he had to update Max about: his invention, Witch Hazel, the secret map, his restored imagination and, best of all, staying up all night for the second time in his life.

Today they would plan their strategy to return to the Kingdom of the Merriwarts.

Chapter 7

It took twenty-two rings, but finally Newton stirred from his deep sleep and answered the phone. Max was on the line.

"You sound tired, Newton—you sick? I called earlier but no one answered. Where were you? It's two o'clock in the afternoon. Where's the rest of your family? It's Saturday, what's the deal?"

"Two o'clock! Holy smokes! We've got to hurry. Listen, Max, I don't know how secure this line is, whether or not it's smart to talk over the phone. Are you allowed out of the house?"

"Of course."

"Then, rendezvous here ASAP. Prepare for a mission."

"Will I need any special equipment? Camouflage? Binoculars? Water guns?"

"Yes, yes, yes and yes. And ask your mother for rations. Let her know that you might be gone for a while. If she tries to hug and kiss you, by all means, give her that."

"This sounds serious."

"From here on, we're Code White."

"Roger, wilco. Over and out."

There was so much to do before the portal opened at four o'clock. In a flurry, Newton zipped around his room, gathering essentials, trying not to forget anything. He strapped the wings onto the back of his knapsack. Soon the extra pockets of the knapsack were overflowing and he had to make crucial decisions about what to leave behind. Of course the Polaroid camera was packed. But should he take extra socks or a couple of comic books? (Comic books.) Peanut butter or his cowboy jacket? (Peanut butter.) As he was trying to decide which of his ten flashlights to bring, he heard a noise but couldn't figure out where it was coming from. At first he thought it might be a mouse, but when he got down on his hands and knees and pressed his ear to the floor, Newton was certain someone was shouting. But where? And how? Had his brothers kidnapped a kid and locked him in a secret compartment?

As Newton crawled toward the far corner of the room, the voice became louder and he could make out the faint cries of "Help me! Help!"

"Where are you?" Newton asked, though he couldn't see anyone and felt extremely foolish talking to the walls. He had the sneaking suspicion someone was videotaping the whole thing and would broadcast it later on some reality-TV show.

"In the corner. I'm stuck under the radiator."

Under the radiator? It made no sense.

"Listen," Newton said, "this isn't funny. I'm in a terrible hurry. No one's in the corner."

This time the voice was louder. "Here! Here!" it cried. "Turn to your left." Newton turned. "You're getting closer."

Suddenly Newton thought he saw something wedged behind the radiator leg and the wall. Squeezing his hand between the space, he reached in and felt a hard object.

"That's it, that's me!" the voiced shouted.

"Whatever you are, you're stuck. You won't budge."

"I don't care how you do it, but please get me out of here!"

As soon as Newton attempted to pry out the object with his jackknife, it screamed, "Easy there! I'm made of plastic, not metal!"

"I thought you said you didn't care how I did it."

"I never expected that you'd try to carve me up."

But the knife had loosened the object a bit and after a couple of minutes of jiggling, Newton finally pulled it out.

And was shocked to discover his long-lost action figure, Commander Joe (with one arm missing from the time Engelbert fed it to the dog).

"Newton, where were you these past two years? I've been yelling my head off, hoping someone would rescue me. Do you have any idea how bored I've been?"

Newton felt awful. Next to Mugsy, Commander Joe was his number two favorite toy. They had hunted tigers in Borneo, conquered ant colonies in Nepal and discovered stolen treasures buried deep in the basement. "I'm sorry. I looked everywhere but I couldn't find you." It was true—for weeks Newton had searched but finally had to admit that Joe was lost forever. "How'd you end up under the radiator?"

"The dastardly Engelbert snuck in and snatched me off the shelf before I had a chance to administer body blows. Then, I shudder to even recall, he hammered me into the corner. Oh sure, I fought the best I could, but it was no use. He was too strong, too quick, too evil."

"Engelbert!" Newton gasped. "How could he!"

"All this time you never heard me? I practically grew a new set of vocal cords from yelling."

"No, not until now. Honest. If only I had known where you were. I'm sorry."

Joe paused for a moment, then said, "Aw, forget it, I needed a break from the rat race. Time to recharge the batteries, Pokey."

"Um . . . no one calls me Pokey anymore," Newton informed Joe.

"Right. Of course, Pokey—I mean, Newton. You're all grown up. I can see that." Joe noticed Newton's packed knapsack. "You seem to be in a hurry. Am I interrupting anything?"

"Well . . . as a matter of fact—" Newton began but stopped, unsure whether or not to debrief Joe on his mission. (Joe had a disturbing habit of picking fights with other toys who even so much as looked at him the wrong way. What would he do in the Kingdom of the Merriwarts?) However, Commander Joe and Newton were blood brothers, even if Joe didn't have any blood. And blood brothers never kept secrets from each other. In short, Newton had no choice; he told Joe everything.

"I've never heard of these Merriwarts before," Joe said. "They sure sound like they're in a heap of trouble. Count me in. But still, before we go, shouldn't we set some explosives to blow up the quadruplets? Get rid of them once and for all?"

"There's no time. Besides, I don't think that would be such a good idea."

"Why not?"

"Everyone would know it was me."

Newton had almost finished packing when Max rang the front doorbell. It was two-forty. They would have to walk fast.

Newton gathered the rest of his stuff, tucked Joe in his front pocket and met Max at the door.

In his haste, Newton didn't see the list of fourteen jobs tacked to his bedroom door. His parents wanted him to wash the dishes in the sink before they got back from the baseball game. His brothers had added rewiring the fuse box, laundering the three weeks' worth of dirty clothes that sat in moldy piles in the basement and finishing the jigsaw puzzle that had only twenty-five matches out of a possible eight thousand pieces. Had he read his brothers' dire warning at the bottom of the list, Newton would have realized that if he failed to complete every job he would be dealt with accordingly.

But, as previously mentioned, Newton never saw the list—not that it would have made any difference anyway.

During the two-mile walk to the Owls stadium, Newton updated Max on his adventures. By Max's lack of enthusiastic response, Newton could tell something was bothering him. "What's wrong, Max?"

"Nothing," Max said quickly.

Too quickly.

"Sure there is. I can tell."

"Okay. You're right. It's just that I wish you had flown by and come to pick me up. I would have come to Witch Hazel's for sure. And besides . . ." Max's voice trailed off.

"Besides what?"

"Well, I watched a TV show on UFOs last night, and it sure seems suspiciously similar to what you're talking about. It explained how people can convince themselves of anything—whether it's true or not."

"UFAs. Unidentified Flying Apparitions. Big difference. I never said I saw a UFO."

"I'm sure you saw what you saw," Max said.

Newton couldn't believe he was having this argument with Max. The portal was set to open in twenty minutes and they were still a half-mile away from the stadium. "You're saying you don't believe me?" he challenged.

Max fidgeted. He would do that—scratch the back of his neck, rub his toe in the dirt, pull on his earlobe, knock his knees together. "I believe that you believe it," Max said.

"What about Herbert the giant and the Kingdom of the Merriwarts?"

"Well . . . I was reconsidering that too. Did you ever think that maybe you dreamed it?"

"*Dreamed it!*" Newton shouted. "You just don't have dreams like that!"

"Okay, okay. But do you really expect me to believe that leprechauns exist?" Max asked diplomatically. "That monsters haunt houses? Imaginations can be restored? Witch Hazel doesn't eat kids?"

The portal was set to open in eighteen minutes. "That's exactly what I'm telling you," Newton replied.

"Then, how come you're the only one who's seen any of this?"

Newton was confused. What was bothering Max? Suddenly he had an inspiration. With a flourish

Newton pulled Commander Joe out of his breast pocket.

"Where'd you find Joe? I thought he was lost," Max exclaimed.

"I wasn't lost. I was a POW, you moron," Joe piped up sarcastically.

"Relax, Joe," Newton warned, then turned to Max and whispered, "You know how he can be a little gruff sometimes."

Max was confused. "Who can be gruff?"

"Commander Joe."

"Newton, are you okay?"

"Sure. Why?"

"You're talking to an action figure like it was real."

"I am real! Doesn't he understand I'm a government-trained covert operations specialist?"

Newton was embarrassed and told Joe to calm down.

"But I am calm," Max replied.

"No, not you. I was talking to Joe."

"But Joe can't talk, he's only a toy."

Newton had to hold Joe back from leaping on Max. "*Only a toy*! Come on, punk! Let's dance!" he yelled, holding his fist up, ready to go toe-to-toe with Max.

Newton shoved Commander Joe back in his

pocket before the figure could utter another word. "I'm sorry about that, Max."

"Sorry about what?"

"Commander Joe. It's just that he takes things a little too personally."

Max tried to laugh it off, pretending Newton was joking. "That's funny."

Newton could feel Joe kicking against his chest, trying to get out. He ignored Joe. "Didn't you hear him yelling just now, Max?"

"No, because he wasn't yelling. In fact, he wasn't doing anything at all. The joke's over. Stop pretending."

Pretending? Newton was shocked. This wasn't what he had expected from Max. He didn't know how to reply. Newton took a deep breath and counted to ten. "Max, are you telling me that you think I'm *pretending* Commander Joe can talk?"

"What I can't figure out is why you need to lie to me. After all, aren't we supposed to be best friends? Then again, maybe I don't know you as well as I thought I did. You didn't come by my house last night . . ."

"I've already apologized for that," Newton replied softly, dread starting to creep up the back of his throat.

"Listen, why don't we forget about the portal for today? We could see a movie or hang out at my house. Or maybe test your invention."

"I can't do that, Max," Newton said, looking at his watch. "Time is running out. I need to go back to the Merriwarts. The portal is opening in sixteen minutes. Are you with me or not?"

Max rubbed the toe of his sneaker along the ground. He coughed weakly, dramatically, mostly for effect. "I'm not sure I'm feeling so great."

"What's the matter? You got a cold or something?"

"Yeah, I think so," Max replied rather unconvincingly. He kept his head down, staring at his feet, and would not look up at Newton. "Bad timing. I'm sorry."

And then, because they were best friends, both realized that nothing else needed to be said. Their misunderstanding hung in the air like a stink bomb set to explode. It made Newton feel sad and lonely, searching for another way to explain. But he knew that if Max didn't believe him by now, he never would.

"Well, if you've got a cold, you really should go."

"That's probably the smart thing to do," Max

replied, and started walking away. He turned back and said gently, "I could talk to my mother about your insanity. Maybe she knows someone who could get you psychiatric help—a lobotomy or something so that you won't hear the voices anymore."

Then Max left.

"Yeah," Newton said, even though Max couldn't hear him. "And we don't need to test my invention. It works. I would know." Newton was sadder and lonelier than he could ever remember feeling. He had fourteen minutes to make it to the portal and he couldn't move.

Soon Joe was squirming in his pocket like a kernel in a popcorn maker, demanding to be let out. As soon as he was released, Joe said dramatically, "Then there were two." He gave Newton a roundhouse to the chest. "Chin up, Pokey, what's the game plan now?"

"My name's not Pokey and I don't have a game plan."

"Come on, Newton, we've got to get going if we want to make the portal in time."

But Newton just stood there motionless—like he was intending on growing roots. So Joe climbed up his shoulder, grabbed Newton's earlobe and started swinging.

"Cut it out, Commander Joe," Newton demanded, trying to pull him off. Joe, who had an even stronger Chinese Death Grip than Engelbert, refused to release the lobe and continued to annoy Newton.

"Newton, we've got to go."

"I don't feel like it anymore, seeing as how Max doesn't believe me."

"So what? Who cares? You two have a difference of opinion right now, a dip in the roller coaster of life. But the important thing is to stay focused. Max will come around eventually. Trust me."

"How do you know?" Newton asked, starting to feel slightly better.

"Because best friends always do." Joe looked at his watch. "Come on, Pokey, we've really, really, really got to go! T minus eight minutes!"

"Eight minutes!" Newton shouted, surprised. "We might not make it!"

Joe insisted on perching on Newton's shoulder as they sprinted toward the stadium. With less than three and a half minutes before the portal opened, Newton climbed the right-field fence, expecting to continue directly into the stadium without stopping.

However, halfway up the links he made an awful discovery—the stadium was full! How could Newton have forgotten? Because this was the seventh and deciding game in the epic series between the hometown Owls and their arch-rivals, the Reds, there wasn't an empty seat in the house. Newton looked around frantically—and saw his family sitting directly behind home plate.

What was he supposed to do, call a time-out and slip under home plate when no one was watching?

Newton looked at the scoreboard. The game was tied with two out in the bottom of the ninth. With the bases empty, the batter, Homer Jones (whose real name was Chester Jones but he was called Homer because he had never hit a home run in his career) was staring at a 2–1 count. Homer had a lifetime batting average of .169 and no one in the stadium was too optimistic about his chances of a hit. The game would go into extra innings.

Whoever controlled the portals had a lousy sense of timing.

Newton pulled out the map again to confirm that this was the right place. It was.

T minus two minutes, forty-five seconds. "What are we going to do, Joe?"

"I ran into a similar situation once during an expedition in the jungles of Zaire. An elephant herd was about to stampede us and we needed to become invisible in a hurry."

"What'd you do?"

"The last thing I remember is a giant foot about to squash me."

"That's helpful," Newton replied, then tried to concentrate, willing a flurry of mental gymnastics. But his brain cramped and he was no closer to figuring out a distraction. Seconds melted away.

The pitcher threw a strike right down the pipe; the batter, frozen like a statue, just watched it sail by him. The umpire yelled, "Strrriiiike twooo!"

Straddling the top of the fence, twelve feet off the ground, Newton knew there was only one distraction that could save him. Homer had to hit the ball.

Even with that remote possibility, making it to the portal was a long shot, a lottery at best. "As soon as the ball is hit, I'm running," he told Joe. "Fair or foul, we go. No one will expect it."

"I like your kamikaze style, Pokey."

The pitcher wound up again, this time putting everything he had behind the throw. The batter never saw the ball. The catcher barely saw the ball. The umpire (distracted by an ant climbing up his neck) didn't see the ball at all. And so, what was a certain strike was called outside. The house was full. The count was three and two. There was less than a minute before the portal opened.

Newton took out his binoculars and scanned the crowd. He saw that the Wiggins family had collectively inched closer to the edge of their seats. He guessed that by now Ernest had finished biting all his fingernails—that's why he had removed his shoes and socks and was gnawing on his toes. That by the movement of Earl's lips he was fervently trying to hex the pitcher. That Eric had begun counting to distract himself, but would get confused and have to start all over again before he reached ten—

Engelbert had picked up a pair of binoculars—

And was staring straight at Newton. They locked binoculars across the field. Newton saw Engelbert nudge his brothers and point at him.

As the pitcher wound up, four heads turned away from Newton. The stadium went silent, an expectant mass of bodies all staring, waiting and watching for a little white ball to leave the pitcher's hand.

And the throw was delivered.

The pitch came right down the center of the plate—another fastball, except this one had more heat on it than a three-alarm burrito. The batter swung and, miracle of miracles, somehow managed to connect wood to leather. A great roar went up. Every neck in the stadium craned to follow the rising hit.

Newton took off for home plate as soon as the ball left the bat. He landed on the field running, his head down in an all-out dash for the portal. No one in the stadium, except for the quadruplets and, unfortunately for the Reds, their right fielder, UpJaw MacGraw from Witchita, noticed him streak across the grass.

UpJaw had backed up all the way past the warning track, but he knew the ball did not have enough juice to soar out of the stadium. Perfectly positioned to make the catch (and send the game into extra innings), Newton momentarily distracted UpJaw. And that's all it took. The break in concentration was enough to cause him to lose sight of the ball. And what had been a certain catch scuffed the side of his glove before dropping to the ground.

Homer, who had more speed than a jackrabbit on sugar, was already at second base.

Newton was sprinting—though the wings slowed him.

The quadruplets were out of their seats, scrambling to get on the field and stop their brother from once again disgracing the family.

The crowd, who could barely believe Homer Jones had hit the ball, much less swallow the fact that UpJaw MacGraw had dropped it, still didn't notice Newton.

Commander Joe, perched on Newton's neck, shouted, "Go! Go! Go!" He would have slapped Newton like a thoroughbred to speed him up, but since he had only one arm, he needed it to cling onto Newton's shirt.

UpJaw MacGraw from Witchita was still in a daze, looking to the umpires for some kind of ruling about a kid running across the field.

Homer Jones rounded second with one thought in his mind: Make it to home.

By now Newton was past the shortstop, headed for exactly the same place.

The quadruplets were on top of the visiting team's dugout and also closing fast on home plate.

UpJaw shook himself out of his daze, picked up the ball and hurled it toward home plate.

The throw came at the catcher like a rocket.

The third-base coach waved Homer on. Newton was past the pitcher's mound. Homer continued pumping toward home.

"T-minus six seconds!" Joe yelled.

Newton could see a crack of light under home plate. The quadruplets flew off the top of the dugout with the sole intention of clearing a path for Homer.

Homer dove.

Newton dove.

The quadruplets dove.

The catcher braced himself.

The umpire positioned himself.

The fans prepared themselves.

The ball continued hurtling through the air.

Homer Jones, the ball and the quadruplets all arrived at home plate at precisely the same time—colliding into each other, and into the catcher and umpire who were already crowding the tiny piece of real estate.

Newton, fortunately, had misjudged his slide and ended up a foot short of his goal, licking dirt. Between the sprawled bodies he saw the portal opening under the plate.

Newton had his chance! He crawled forward, rolled the umpire off the plate, pushed aside the dazed catcher and, without a moment's hesitation, jumped in the portal.

The portal closed behind him, but not before someone else had slipped through—the same someone who had seen Newton fly back into his house last night.

Someone who was very interested in a boy who could build wings.

Chapter 8

"Where are we?" Commander Joe asked, looking around in amazement.

Newton had no idea. The portal had deposited them on top of a boulder as big as an iceberg. This was definitely not the forest Newton had arrived at on his previous visit. Did Witch Hazel give them the wrong directions? The landscape was prehistoric and Newton would not have been surprised to see a T. rex or stegosaurus strutting by. As far as he could see, huge craters pocked the landscape. If the situation weren't so dire, with minimal effort and a shovel, Newton felt he might unearth some spectacular geological samples.

Newton shivered even though the sun burned brightly and the air was warm. Something didn't feel quite right, though he could not say what was giving him such a dreadful case of ants-in-the-pants. He examined his wings and found they were still intact from the play at home plate and the portal journey. Quickly he began to assemble his invention, in a hurry to become airborne, without any good reason for the rush.

"Slow down, Pokey. What's our plan?" Joe asked. "Where are all these giants I've heard so much about? Maybe Max was right to think you're going insane."

"Help me with the pulleys. We'll see if we can find the forest from the air. PS, FYI, put a zipper on further insane comments."

"Relax. I was kidding. By the way, speaking of certified, do you have a license to operate an aviation vehicle? I only ask because, as a former Class II instructor, I can't let you take off unless you cough up some documentation."

"How can I be certified for an invention that is not even patented?"

"Touché. Though I'm not sure I agree with your logic, since we're Code White, I'll turn a blind eye this time," Joe replied, then darted around, securing ropes and checking the lines. Because he was so small, he could untangle lines with the efficiency of a puppeteer.

Halfway through reviewing the pre-flight checklist, the boulder they were standing on shifted. "Did you feel that?" Joe asked. Before Newton could reply, the rock heaved dramatically, then began vibrating. Earthquake? Fault lines?

"Strap yourself in, Joe, we're taking off," Newton ordered. The vibration grew louder, angrier, sounding like a swarm of bees. Newton definitely wanted to be airborne.

"Roger, Captain," Commander Joe replied, and jumped into Newton's front pocket. With Joe securely tucked in, Newton began flapping. But although the wings went up and down, he could not achieve liftoff.

Joe looked up at Newton. "What's going on?"

"Something must be wrong with the motor," Newton shouted, for the noise had increased, the boulder roaring like a race car set to start the Indy 500. Newton's knees shook and his teeth chattered and his head started hurting from the constant rumbling. If the motor was broken beyond repair they were in deep, deep trouble.

"Leave it to me," Joe barked, scurrying out of his front pocket, over Newton's shoulder and into the knapsack. "Everything seems to be ship shape," Joe yelled.

The boulder started to roll. "J-J-Joe," Newton stuttered, barely able to utter a word over the vibration. "P-p-please hurry." As if pushed by an invisible hand, the boulder began to move—at first slowly, then picking up speed so that Newton had to jog just to stay atop it. To make matters worse, Newton saw that all of the other boulders around them had also started to roll. It was only a matter of time before they began smashing into one another like a convention of mad sumo wrestlers. Twice their boulder had narrowly missed colliding with another.

"I'm trying. I can't figure out why—"

Crash! Bam! Pow!

"Ouch!" Newton didn't even see the rock that hit them from behind. He fell hard on the boulder, scraping an unhealthy strip of skin off both shins but somehow avoiding crushing his wings.

"Commander Joe! Commander Joe!" Newton yelled, hoping his friend was still alive.

"It's a good thing my brain is made from reinforced plastic. I'm all right, Pokey!" Newton heard Joe's muffled reply. He was still buried inside the knapsack.

At least the collision had temporarily halted the boulder's progress. But because it was still vibrating, Newton couldn't stand up, and began shaking toward the edge. "I c-c-can't h-h-hold on much l-l-long-g-g-ger."

Clinging to the rock, Newton wondered how in the name of perilous situations he had ever ended up here. What leap of logic had made him believe that trying to save a group of giants (who may or may not have been figments of his fragile imagination) was something he could accomplish? Newton always thought of himself as a boy more prone to the leisurely pursuits: inventing, reading, playing video games, watching television, sleeping. In fact, tree climbing was the only physical exercise he actually enjoyed. So how did he end up in the midst of an adventure that would make a superhero squirm? For someone supposedly so smart, how could he be so stupid? A delicious vision of himself at home, hiding in his attic, eating peanut butter crackers and reading the latest issue of *Inventors Quarterly*, floated in his brain.

Two events simultaneously brought Newton out of his daydream. The first was Commander Joe's triumphant shouts signaling his discovery that the pin connecting the solar rotor to the main pulley had been pulled out.

The second was Newton losing his handhold on the boulder. "Connect it, Joe! We're falling fast!" Newton shouted.

The ground rushed squashingly closer.

"I've almost got it! I've almost got it!" Joe relayed.

Newton knew they wouldn't make it and closed his eyes.

Joe was yelling triumphantly in his ear. "They didn't certify me SAS—Secret Agent Superstar—for nothing! One-armed and upside down I did it! Flap, Pokey, flap!"

Newton flapped hard enough to make a hummingbird jealous, but it was too little too late. There wasn't nearly enough room to slow down and start ascending. In horror Newton realized they had an unavoidable rendezvous with terra very firma.

At the moment of impact, just as they were preparing themselves for life-ending squishification, a huge roar went up and the ground spilt, instantly creating a gaping crevice. Miraculously, they continued downward into a black hole. The air was cool and invigorating, and Newton never stopped beating his wings, scarcely able to comprehend his good fortune (though he fully expected at any moment to be gored by a piece of jagged rock).

Somewhere in the depths of darkness, they stopped their terrifying descent, avoiding any catastrophes, before beginning a considerably calmer upward journey. With only the light from the opening to guide him, Newton was deathly afraid he'd clip his wings or that the opening would close before they made it out.

It didn't happen. Once outside, navigating his way through the minefield of moving boulders proved tricky, but soon Newton and Joe found themselves high above the seismic mess, aware of just how lucky they had been to escape.

"Great work on fixing the pin. You were incredible under pressure."

"Just doing my job," Joe replied from his perch on Newton's head. Secretly he was tickled pink (or in his case, flesh-tone paint number 334). "For a while there, I thought we were deader than Thanksgiving turkeys."

Newton scanned the horizon. "Any idea which direction we should go?"

Joe retrieved Witch Hazel's map. But they opened it to discover it had gone completely blank. There wasn't even a single portal showing. Without landmarks or a map to guide them, they were lost.

"Looks like we're up the stream without a compass," Joe remarked.

Newton was worried but tried not to show it. He reminded himself to stay calm. There were worse things in the world than being completely lost. "When they gave you SAS training, did it include navigation without maps?"

"Nope," Joe replied.

"Well then, we're going to have to make a decision. Do you have any suggestions?" Newton asked hopefully.

"Nope. Your guess is as good as mine," Joe said.

After much hemming and hawing and a bit of debating, they decided to follow the sun. At least that way they could be sure they weren't traveling in circles.

* * *

Hours later Newton was still flying. By gliding he was able to give his arms a rest, but they were getting tired and still there was no sign of the Merriwarts or their forest. Newton wondered whether Witch Hazel had mistakenly sent them to the wrong portal. Joe was sleeping, snoring like a dog trying to suck the last few drops out of a milk shake, and Newton had time to think about the curious mystery of the missing pin in his solar engine. By his calculations it was impossible that the pin had come loose. So secure was the piece of machinery that the only explanation was deliberate sabotage. But who? And when? And why? It made no sense, and yet, Newton could feel it was true.

Someone or something out there was onto them in a most diabolical way.

Eventually Newton and Joe put the Land of the Boulders behind them. As they flew, the terrain changed from flat to rolling until they were over a mountain range. But these mountains soon became savage, sheer-faced outcroppings without a speck of vegetation or sign of life anywhere. The farther they flew into the range, the higher they were forced to climb in order to scale each peak. Icicles had formed on the tips of his wings and Newton's face was starting to turn blue with cold. His fingers were numb, movement in his toes a fading memory. The sun was setting and soon they would have to abandon flying and find a spot to land for the night—a thought neither Newton nor Joe had much appetite for, considering the inhospitable nature of the area. To complicate matters, Newton was weak with hunger. The exertion of flying was leaving him dangerously exhausted.

"I'll try to make it over this last mountain and then we'll have to land," Newton told Joe.

Near the summit, his arms began aching and his shoulders grew numb. He told himself, "Just five more flaps, then I'll rest." After five flaps he repeated the mantra and kept going. To stop would mean defeat. The higher they flew, the more the winds howled, trying to push Newton back. It took every last iota of energy Newton could muster not to give up.

But as soon as he crested the mountain, Newton realized the effort had been worth it. Far below was a green valley and through the dusk Newton thought he saw a cabin. On his descent, as he spiraled lower and lower, Newton was so overcome with fatigue that all he wanted to do was tuck in his wings and nose-dive for the ground. Wisely he never gave in to the impulse, and Joe stomped on his shoulders to keep the blood flowing.

The cabin came into focus, smoke curling up from the chimney. As Newton flew lower he heard music pouring out of the windows and smelled the appealing aroma of baked goods. For two exhausted travelers it was an oasis, an inviting place to rest.

Perhaps too inviting.

Newton was all for flying right through the front door (only slightly bigger than human-size) but Joe instructed him to land away from the cabin. "Hopefully we haven't been spotted yet," he warned. "That way we can survey the situation before committing ourselves. If there's one thing I've learned about strangers, it's that, until proven otherwise, they're strange."

So Newton touched down behind an evergreen. Though the trees weren't as humongous as those in the Merriwart forest, they were certainly gigantic by Earth standards. For the first few minutes, all Newton could do was lie splayed on the ground, exhausted, unable to move, gasping for breath. But the combination of Joe pulling his neck hairs and the irresistible smell of baked cookies soon got him on his feet.

Stealthily they tiptoed toward the cabin.

As they were about to peer in the window, the oddest thing happened. A huge, brightly colored bird swooped over them so quickly and so silently that Newton wasn't sure if the movement was imagined.

"Did you see that?" Newton asked. The bird seemed familiar—it looked like Herbert's bird, Margaret.

"See what?"

"Nothing," Newton replied.

When Newton and Joe turned back again to look in the window they were met with the most fantastic sight of all: food.

It was as if some inspired cook had read Newton's mind and concocted dishes that met his every desire (and in extra-large portions). Sugary treats were piled like books in a library. Pies, cookies, tarts, syrups, milk shakes—you name it, there seemed to be an appetizing plate of it inside the cabin.

Before Joe could make sure this wasn't a trap, Newton ran around to the front of the house and knocked on the door. "Newton, wait," Joe warned, but Newton kept knocking excitedly.

"Did you see all that food?"

"Yeah, but don't you think—"

"I wonder if they have any marshmallow pie!"

"Pokey, I'm worried that—"

"And cookies. And butter tarts. And did you notice if there were any Choclairs?"

"Newton, we should—"

"Can you believe our luck? This is extraordinary. We need food and they have food. What are the chances of that?"

Though Newton continued to knock on the door, no one answered.

Joe, who never got hungry because his inventors had cleverly filled his stomach with plastic, had the heebie-jeebies. "Newton, maybe we should leave. Frankly, I'm worried. Why would there be a cabin filled with all this stuff in the middle of nowhere?"

Newton put a hand up. "Joe, I don't want to hear it. Either I eat or I will die." Newton's mind had narrowed its focus so much that all he could think about was the smorgasbord awaiting him on the other side of the door. What would he start with? An ice-cream sandwich? A dozen peanut butter cookies? Perhaps a pound of chocolate as an hors d'oeuvre.

"I can't wait any longer," Newton declared, then turned the handle. The door opened. "Hello? Is anyone home?" he asked as soon as he stepped inside.

The house was silent.

Whoever owned the cabin was gone.

Intoxicated by the smell of food, Newton began eating. To be fair, he only intended to take a few unnoticed samples—a pull of taffy, a nibble of a candy-cane cookie—until the owner returned. After all, Newton prided himself on his manners. But it only took a bite of pound cake to put Newton in full glutton mode. So fast and so furiously did he cram food in his mouth that if it had been an eating contest, he might have broken a world record. The food was shove-in-your-mouth delicious and the more Newton ate, the more he wanted to eat. Soon his face was a sticky mess and gunk dribbled down his chin and his shirt was plastered with stains—in short, it was a most disgusting display of eating etiquette, even for a ten-year-old boy.

Newton never even heard Joe's cries to leave room for breakfast.

Newton couldn't stop eating. His cheeks bulged, his earlobes sagged and his stomach grew bigger.

And bigger. And bigger. And bigger. The skin was stretched white until Newton looked like he was nine months pregnant (with triplets).

Joe looked disgusted, then horror-struck, and frantically tried everything he could to get Newton to stop eating, but it was no use.

Newton was out of control.

After munching his way through the tub of butterscotch fudge without so much as a burp, Newton tossed back two dozen cupcakes like they were jelly beans.

It was while he was reaching down to scrape out the last remaining wisps of cotton candy from the fifty-pound barrel that disaster struck.

Newton completely seized up.

Every last fiber in his body froze. Nothing moved. It was as if he had turned into a human Popsicle.

"Newton!" he heard Joe shout, but he was unable to answer back. What had happened? He watched Joe scramble up to his face (hanging on by Newton's nostril) and feel for a breath. But Newton knew he wasn't breathing. His lungs had taken a vacation and his windpipe felt like it was in knots. Most alarming of all, Newton's eyes were wide open, his bulging eyeballs straining to arrive at some unknown destination. He desperately wanted to blink but he couldn't make his brain command his eyelids.

Though Joe had received first aid training during his infantry duty in the Great Toy War of '79, Newton knew this was beyond anything he had ever encountered. Newton watched helplessly as every medical procedure Joe tried failed to generate a response. Newton felt himself go colder by the minute. It was only a matter of time before all his systems shut down permanently.

Suddenly Newton heard a great crashing, but of course was unable to turn and discover the cause. He then saw a huge hand fishing around. The hand scattered dishes, turned over furniture, scratched the walls and broke a couple of windows before grabbing Newton and hauling him outside. Out of the corner of his eye, Newton saw Joe jump into his front pocket.

Once outside, Newton realized he was spinning, that whoever had grabbed him was swinging him around furiously. If Newton actually had the ability to feel anything, he suspected the activity would make him incredibly dizzy. At amusement parks, he always made it a rule to avoid spinny rides.

At one point, Newton thought he saw Joe fly out

of his pocket and rocket into the bushes, but he couldn't be sure. The world had become a whirling blur.

And then it happened. Again. Newton blew chunks. Food spewed out of him like a volcano, vomit flying in all directions, covering trees, painting the ground Technicolor gross. As he continued to swing, Newton continued to hurl, a fire hose of upchuck.

Then, as suddenly as he had started barfing, Newton stopped. Then whoever was spinning

Newton put him on the ground, though the world continued to rotate wickedly fast.

Newton found he could move again, that his body wasn't stone, though he was in no shape to stand up.

He tried to focus on the creature who had been spinning him, but the world still seemed like it was whirling around, and Newton couldn't get a good look. He vaguely saw a giant figure stagger, then trip on a root and topple violently to the ground, unable to make even the feeblest attempt to break his fall.

A loud *crack* shot through the forest as the giant's head made contact with a rock. Newton winced and wondered if brains would splatter everywhere.

The giant was still.

The night was still.

Before Newton passed out, he saw Joe sprinting toward him.

Chapter 9

"Wake up, Pokey! Don't go into the white light! Come back! We need you!" Newton heard Joe urging. His friend sounded like he was very far away.

Newton cautiously opened his eye.

But quickly had to shut it again because the world was still rotating wickedly fast.

"What happened, Joe? I feel awful," Newton groaned.

"You pigged out, soldier. It was disgusting."

Then Joe told him all the details (especially the part about Newton refusing to listen to his warnings). Joe told Newton how he had not stirred for hours, although his body had shrunk back to its normal size. All the while Joe had tried to remain positive, but couldn't help but ponder the dreadful possibility that Newton might be past the point of no return.

Nonetheless he had continued to troop up and down Newton's face, hoping for signs of life. The temperature had dropped and Joe feared an enemy attack, though at least the moon gave off enough light that he could monitor the bushes.

It was while Joe was cresting Newton's nose for the two hundred and twelfth time that he finally noticed the flutter of an eyelid. Which was followed by another flutter. "And here we are," Joe concluded.

"Thanks," Newton said weakly but sincerely.

"Just doing a soldier's duty," Joe replied gruffly, afraid to show any affection out in the field.

When Newton was finally able to stand (by keeping his woozy head extremely still), he walked unsteadily over to the giant.

And discovered, lying there, none other than Herbert, knocked out colder than a winter day at the North Pole.

As time passed, Newton gradually started feeling better and his appetite returned, though he dared not go near the cabin. As for Herbert, he was breathing but no amount of prodding or pulling could wake him up. Newton and Joe kept vigil, worried that their only hope of escape had slipped into a Rip Van Winkle coma.

Desperate, bored and growing increasingly suspicious that they were being watched, Joe grabbed one of Herbert's nose hairs and began pulling, rationalizing that if the Nostril Torture Method didn't kick-start consciousness, nothing would, and they might as well leave him. The hairs were like ropes, and Joe pretended it was a tug-of-war (although considerably grosser), straining with all his might, extracting one coarse hair at a time. Near exhaustion, while pulling out the sixth hair, Joe didn't notice Herbert's nostril twitch. Before you could say "*Gesundheit*," Herbert let out a monstrous sneeze that sent Joe shooting through the air like a bottle rocket. He landed headfirst in the mud. Newton rushed over and pulled him out.

"Great boogers! I think he slimed me," Joe said, trying to clean himself off.

Meanwhile, Herbert, after some moaning and some groaning, some complaining and some general crankiness, declared, "I feel like dirt," and unsteadily sat up. The rock he had landed on was still embedded in his skull. He pulled the stone off and examined it. "This would explain the headache," he self-diagnosed.

"Are you all right?" Newton asked. "I mean, the side of your head is caved in."

"Oh, I'll be fine. I always pass out after the De-Glutton Maneuver. Why I don't just sit down and wait it out, I'll never know."

"The De-Glutton Maneuver?"

Herbert explained how Margaret, his rainbow eagle, while out on patrol, had discovered Newton looking in at the Cabin of Gluttony. She remembered him from his last visit to the Kingdom of the Merriwarts. Unsure whether Newton was a friend or foe, Margaret flew back to warn Herbert.

The giant immediately realized Newton would be in serious trouble if help didn't arrive at once. For all along the undefended border between the Land of Nothing and the land of the Merriwarts were spaced similar Cabins of Gluttony, tempting unsuspecting travelers like Newton. The cabins were nothing more than ingenious security checks to be avoided at all costs. For, as Newton had experienced, once a person started eating, a complex chemical reaction known as Sugar Petrifaction set in, eventually shutting down all systems. Later,

Merriwart patrols would then find out who had been secretly trying to enter their kingdom.

"Fortunately," Herbert said, "I managed to de-gluttonize you before the effects were irreversible. Now tell me, what are you doing back here? I thought Margaret permanently sealed the attic portal after your last visit."

"Sealed the portal? Why?"

"So you wouldn't come back. Us Merriwarts are very particular about visitors. How did you get back?"

Newton told Herbert all of the details about Witch Hazel, about the baseball game and arriving in the Land of the Boulders. Then, uncertain how to proceed, he took a deep breath and told the giant about the conversation he had overheard between Prince Natas and his brother, about their plans for the Merriwart forest.

Herbert seemed dubious. "That's ridiculous. Why would anyone cut down a tree? Trees are part of our family. Besides, the Liveds are our friends. They're going to give us water."

"I'm only a kid, and apparently I have an over-active imagination, so I might be wrong, but that's what I heard and that's what I came all this way to warn you about."

Herbert's ears wiggled, fluttering like wings, as he thought about what Newton had said, a sure sign he was suspicious. "How do I know you're not lying?"

Lying? What was wrong with these giants? Perhaps Merriwarts were a little too distrustful for their own good. "Listen, Herbert, I'm hungry, tired, scared and more than a little homesick. If you don't believe me, fine, show me the way out of here and I'll gladly be on my way. I promise, you'll never see me again."

Herbert didn't seem to like Newton's tone. It was far too saucy. He bent down to look in Newton's eyes, searching for any signs of deception.

Joe, who had regained his position on Newton's shoulder, waved his hand in front of his face. "Gas mask time or what! Back off, beast breath, you're making me sick."

Herbert either ignored Joe or didn't hear him as he continued to stare at Newton, as if trying to go past his eyeballs into his brain. Newton felt like squirming under the intense gaze, but remained still.

Finally Herbert declared, "There's something else you're not telling me. I'm certain of it."

"What, are you a mind reader?"

"Obviously not or I'd know exactly what you were thinking. But Merriwarts are known for their excellent sense of hunch and right now mine's buzzing on high alert. Besides, your tear ducts are watering in a way that I don't entirely trust."

If they had such an excellent sense of hunch, why hadn't they sniffed out the lies of Natas and his brother? Newton wondered, but decided against bringing up the point. Should Newton tell Herbert about the quadruplets? What if the giant was offended? What if he refused?

"Well, I was sort of hoping . . ." Newton paused. "I know this sounds silly, but I thought maybe if I helped save your kingdom, you might do me a favor in return." Then in a rush, before he chickened out, Newton explained to Herbert about his brothers and their murderous ways. "I'm pretty sure if you, as my protector, stuck your arm into their room in the middle of the night, growled fiercely through the window a couple of times, warned them to be nice to me, stomped around and let them know all about your favorite quadruplet torture techniques, they just might stop bullying me."

Herbert harrumphed. "So, you take me for a thug. A brute. An intimidator. A common bully.

Oh sure, I might not be as educated as some, but I have sophisticated tastes. I'm not common!"

"No! No!" Newton replied. "I'm not saying you are. Don't get me wrong, it could be any giant. It's just that I'm sure they'd respond to size in a way they don't respond to anything else."

"So *any* giant will do! Well, that makes me feel *sooo* much better. I don't think so."

Joe piped up, "Something's oozing out of your head."

Herbert squinted. Because of his nearsightedness he couldn't see the action figure. "Did someone say something?"

"I did," Joe declared. Newton held Joe inches from Herbert's face until he came into focus.

The giant was amazed. "I've seen gnats bigger than you. Who would have guessed such small people existed."

"Who would have guessed giants could be so ugly," Joe shot back, extra-sensitive to any references to his size, then bit Herbert on the finger.

"Joe!" Newton yelled, quickly pulling him off.

For a moment Newton was worried that Herbert was going to squash Joe like a ladybug, but instead he laughed. "That tickled. You're pretty funny, squirt."

A glob of sticky green slime seeping from Herbert's head landed on Joe's head. "Hey, you've already slimed me once. Have some pride in yourself and wipe it up!" Joe ordered.

Herbert felt the side of his skull. Sure enough, he had a rather severe brain drain situation. Scooping up a handful of mud, he packed it over the wound. "No wonder I felt a draft," he said, not in the least bothered by Margaret, who had flown over to peck at remnants of green gunk that hadn't been covered.

Herbert looked up at the night sky as if it were a clock, then announced, "Well, gentlemen, I must be off. It's been a pleasure saving your lives." The giant started walking away.

Alarmed, Newton called after him, "Where are you going? What about the Liveds?"

"There's nothing I can do. Didn't I tell you? They've kicked me out of the trees. Have a nice night." Before Newton could get another word in, Herbert disappeared, the woods swallowing him into darkness.

"That's one weird giant," Joe declared. "I say we forget about the Merriwarts and make plans to head home."

Joe's suggestion wasn't such a bad one, assuming

they could actually find a way back. But since Newton had no idea where they were and was in no mood to spend the night alone in the forest (even with an overconfident SAS-trained action figure), he made a decision. "Herbert is our only chance—without him we're doomed. If we hope ever to see another Christmas, eat another hot dog, ride another pachyderm in India, we've got to persuade him to help us."

Fortunately, the moon squeezed through the branches and offered just enough light to guide their pursuit.

"Well, let's follow the smell," Joe suggested. "Put me on your shoe so I can track the scent better."

Joe clung to Newton's ankle, sniffing the air. Herbert smelled so bad, he was able to track the giant like a bloodhound tracks a fox. Newton kept up a brisk pace, sensing that they were falling ever farther behind, wondering if they were going in circles, but Joe dismissed any doubts.

"Just turn where I tell you, Pokey. Don't think. You're far too hungry to reason."

By the time Newton was convinced they had all but lost Herbert, he was staggering with hunger and exhaustion, barely able to distinguish a left turn from a right. Joe ordered him to halt. "The oaf's in there," he assured Newton, pointing to a cave, the entrance of which was covered with an animal fur.

"Are you certain?" Newton asked, afraid that if Joe was wrong, he would burst into a den of murderous ogres or Merriwarts who ate boys.

"Of course. But to be safe, so we don't have a repeat of the Cabin of Gluttony, I'll scout the situation out. This is where size, or lack of it, comes in handy. You wait behind that bush. As soon as the coast is clear, I'll give you the signal."

"What's the signal?"

"If I told you, that would take all the fun out of it. Trust me, you'll know it when it comes." And Joe hopped off Newton's ankle and ran to the entrance, then rolled under the fur door.

Which left Newton alone in a strange land, behind a strange bush, looking at strange stars in a strange sky. Twigs cracked, branches groaned, unseen and unknown animals howled and hooted. Newton wondered if one of these sounds was Joe's signal and he just wasn't recognizing it.

Newton waited. And waited. And waited. When he could stand it no longer, he decided to enter the cave. Stealthily he crept toward the entrance, listening for sounds of torture, sniffing for burned plastic, expecting to see mutilated toy parts, but instead he heard, smelled and saw nothing. At the entrance Newton hesitated, still expecting at the last moment to hear Joe's signal.

He didn't. And so he slowly, silently pulled back the animal fur and peered in. Expecting the worst, he was surprised to see that the cave opened into a huge, comfortable room where Herbert was sitting before a fire of lava rocks, cooking. As soon as Newton walked in, Herbert turned and casually said, "It's about time. Dinner's almost ready. I was beginning to think I would have to come out there and drag you in myself. Sit down and we'll eat."

Newton was confused. "You were expecting me?"

"Of course. Why do you think I made so much noise in the forest? I told Margaret you'd be able to follow us, but still, she insisted on circling back just to make sure you hadn't been taken hostage by a troll or two-toed groundling."

Newton decided against telling Herbert that they had tracked him by smell. "So, where's Joe?"

"The little guy? He's not with you?" Herbert asked, surprised.

"No, he snuck in here ages ago to scout things out."

Herbert turned to Margaret, who was perched on a rocky outcropping, and asked if she had seen the action figure. The bird shook her beak. "No, I'm afraid not," Herbert said, "or Margaret would have known. She doesn't miss much."

"But he had to!" Newton exclaimed, starting to panic. "I saw him come in! Maybe Margaret didn't hear him."

The bird cawed indignantly and ruffled her feathers. "Unlikely. Margaret is a rainbow eagle, a breed renowned for its sensory powers. Trust me, the instant your pal entered, she'd know. I'm sorry."

Where had Joe disappeared? Was he hurt? Had something happened to him before he got to the cave? Newton retreated toward the entrance.

"Where are you going?" Herbert asked.

"My friend is missing. We're comrades, I've got to find him."

Herbert grabbed Newton by the ankles and held him upside down—a punishment usually imposed only by the quadruplets. Blood rushed brainward, and his eyeballs bulged. "Put me down!"

"You can't go out there. Not at night. Trust me, leave the cave and you'll never see morning. They'd get you," Herbert calmly added.

"Who are *they*?"

Herbert shuddered. "*They* are the Great Unknown. Creatures more vile and dastardly than our worst nightmare. I'll send Margaret. If Joe's around, she'll find him." With that, Margaret flapped off her perch and disappeared into the darkness.

Herbert put Newton right side up. "Please, sit down. The Toad Horn Pancakes are just about ready. And you know how fickle these things can be." Ignoring protests that Newton was much too worried for food, Herbert handed him a huge plate of pancakes. Staggering under the weight, Newton almost gave himself a hernia and third-degree burns before managing to set the plate on the dirt floor.

And discovered a million squirming horns sticking out from the tops of the pancakes. "Herbert, the pancakes are alive."

"Thank you. It's so hard to know when to stop cooking."

Just to be polite, Newton cut off a piece, closed his eyes, then stuffed the bite in his mouth. The horns tickled his throat before he was able to swallow, but tasted remarkably succulent. To be polite he ate another piece, then another, and another. All the while Herbert watched him closely.

When Newton looked up and discovered that

Herbert wasn't eating he became suspicious. "Why aren't you having any?" He had once seen a movie where the cook poisoned an unsuspecting guest.

"I am a chef. Chefs never eat until the guests are served."

"You're not trying to poison me, are you?"

"Poison you! Is that what you think of my creation!" Herbert raged, and started hurling pots and pans.

"No! No!" Newton cried. "This is delicious! Honest!"

About to send an enormous glass into orbit, Herbert paused. "Delicious? Honestly?"

"This might be the best meal I've ever had," Newton said.

Herbert flared his nostrils and revealed rotten teeth. For a moment Newton was afraid he somehow had re-offended the giant, until he realized the look of alarming ugliness that had spread across the giant's face was in fact a smile.

"Thank you. Obviously you are a boy with extraordinarily refined culinary tastes."

Later, while scrubbing the dishes, Newton finally brought up a question that had been bothering him since he found Herbert in the cave. Namely, what was the giant doing in this inhospitable place? Why wasn't Herbert back with his people in the trees? What had he done to get kicked out of the trees?

At first, Herbert tried to avoid the question by faking a severe case of deafness, but Newton persisted until Herbert finally told him the story—warts and all—of how he came to be banished from the kingdom.

As Herbert explained, the morning after Newton left, Gertrude's engagement was all anyone could talk about. Desperate, Herbert decided to confront Gertrude about his feelings. True love would win the day. Abandoning his Caramelized Gnome Pudding, Herbert snuck out of the kitchen and found Gertrude sitting on the famous Philosopher's Limb, her gold-shoed feet dangling from the branch. Fortunately none of her advisers was around. Herbert dared not sit down beside her, but instead perched a few feet away and poured out his heart (considering he was a giant, it was a waterfall of emotion). The princess never said a word. By the time Herbert was done, he felt like a great burden had been lifted. But when he looked down he discovered that the princess was sound asleep. "I saw the drool coming off her chin, and I knew that we understood each other completely."

"So, why'd you get kicked out?" Newton asked.

Herbert blushed an alarming shade of purple. "Well, that's the embarrassing part." Afraid that Gertrude's advisers might still convince her to marry Prince Natas, Herbert cooked Gertrude the Meal of Seduction—a feast so irresistible that once digested, the eater would forever be smitten with the creator. "Oh sure, it's bending the rules a bit, but we were in love.

"My plan was discovered just as Gertrude was about to dig into dessert. The woe! The heartache!" Herbert wailed dramatically. "Mrs. Hubble was supposed to have the day off, but came into the kitchen, saw all the ingredients and knew what I had done. She rushed into the dining hall and grabbed the dessert as Gertrude was bringing spoon to mouth. Because all four courses weren't consumed, the meal didn't work."

After his arrest and a hasty trial, the elders decreed Herbert be banished for his attempted wooing, forced out of the trees to live on the ground. Though he was still officially in the Kingdom of the Merriwarts, he might as well have been sent to Mars. "For a Merriwart, a life without altitude is like a life without sunshine. I'm miserable. All I want to do is climb up a tree and taste the sky. I miss the leaves. The bark. The branches. My friends. I'm so lonely," Herbert moaned. "To make matters worse, the wedding is set for tomorrow and there's not a thing I can do to stop it. Spurned love will be my eternal burden." Herbert started to wail and the waterworks poured out of both eyes. Newton wondered if all Merriwarts blubbered like babies—or did Herbert have ultra-sensitive tear ducts?

Newton tried to comfort Herbert by rubbing his shin, but that only seemed to make him sadder and the tears come faster and the sobs come louder until the dirt floor was a mucky mess. Newton climbed on a chair to avoid getting stuck in the mud.

As Newton watched Herbert cry, an idea came to him. The plan was so preposterous, such an utter impossibility, that it just might work. When Herbert had moved on to the sniffing phase, Newton took a deep breath and made his pitch: "Listen, Herbert, what if we were to prove that the Liveds were up to no good? That their intentions in marrying Gertrude were less than honorable?"

Herbert blinked a couple of times and wiped snot on his sleeve. "And how do you propose to do that?"

Newton fished in his knapsack, brought out his Polaroid camera and held it before Herbert triumphantly. "With this!"

The giant stared at the strange object in confusion. Obviously, in his hundred and fifty years of life he had never seen anything so . . . foreign. For although Merriwarts were a generally happy race, they were an embarrassingly simple one—a fact they would never own up to. But the tools they used, the homes they built, the clothes they wore were obvious indicators that they hadn't really kept up with the times.

Newton backed up to the far side of the room, until he had all of Herbert's face in the frame, and snapped a photo. Instantly a picture slid out the bottom. Of course, Herbert had no idea what was going on.

Newton handed it to him. "Here," he said.

The giant examined the picture closely, as if expecting the face on the piece of paper to start talking. After a long time he gave the photo back to Newton. "Incredible. Who is the ugly little fellow?"

"It's you," Newton answered.

Herbert laughed. "Funny. No seriously, who is he?"

It took Newton the next hour of explaining and snapping photos of himself and the cave to finally make Herbert understand all about photography. Newton felt bad that in the process he forever altered Herbert's vision of himself as a devilishly handsome, spectacularly dashing young giant.

"I still don't understand how this will prove that the Liveds are evil," Herbert said.

"What if we took photos of the Liveds' kingdom? You know, of trees that had been cut down, fires burning, that sort of thing. If the Merriwarts saw the pictures, wouldn't that prove the Liveds were liars?"

Herbert rubbed his chin. "Imagine the scene—me walking into the Great Hall carrying the proof. The shocked look on everyone's face, the surprise, the horror. I would be a hero, the savior of the Merriwarts. They would sing songs about me and perhaps even give me my own kitchen." He paused and thought about it some more. "You know, Newton, your plan just might work."

Newton was dreading his next question, but went ahead and asked anyway. "Do you have any idea where the Liveds' lair might be?"

As Newton feared, Herbert didn't. Merriwarts hardly ever left their kingdom. There was no reason. Everything they needed could be found in the trees. But as Herbert started sniffing and gulping his way to another round of feeling sorry for himself, a thought, tucked deep in his memory (that fortunately hadn't oozed out when he landed on the rock) started to surface.

"Wait, I'm remembering something." He concentrated very hard until his brain got hold of the memory. "I know who can tell us where to find the Liveds." A long time ago, he told Newton, when he was a boy, his great-great-great-grandmother Rose also had been banished from the trees. "I've been meaning to visit her anyway. You'd like her, Newton, though she's a little on the strange side."

"What'd she get banished for?"

"Family secret, can't talk about it," Herbert declared, as Margaret reappeared, flying to her roost in the time it took Newton to blink. One instant her roost was empty, the next it wasn't.

Sadly the rainbow eagle's search had been unsuccessful. Margaret (as she related to Herbert in caws) had searched everywhere. But she had been unable to locate Commander Joe. Though Newton pestered both Herbert and Margaret, neither could come up with an explanation as to where Joe might have disappeared. It was a mystery that for now no one could explain.

* * *

After drinking a mug of Herbert's Ursa Sassafras Tea, Newton was overcome with tiredness. In spite of his anxiety about Joe, he would need toothpicks to keep his eyelids open. The excitement of the past couple of days finally caught up with him. Even the stench from Herbert's coat (that the giant insisted he use as a bed) couldn't keep Newton awake.

As soon as he lay down, Newton began drifting off. However, before sleep fully washed over him, he made a difficult decision about Joe: If his friend didn't reappear by morning, they would have no choice but to leave without him and find the giantess who could tell them the way to the Liveds' kingdom.

First Max jumped ship and now Joe was missing. Newton had never been lonelier.

Chapter 10

Newton did not sleep long. Not only did Herbert's snoring and Margaret's constant ruffling keep waking him up, but also nightmares invaded his subconscious like ants at a picnic. Twice he awoke shaking and disoriented, in his dreams on the verge of dying a gruesome death or finding Joe melted. By morning his eyes had dark circles, his throat was raw, his head buzzed and he stank from sleeping on Herbert's coat. A quick self-diagnosis revealed that he might have early signs of Spanish flu or bubonic plague. Joe still had not returned and Newton feared fate had dealt his plastic pal a cruel hand.

Even though Gertrude's wedding was to take place at sundown, Herbert insisted on a full breakfast before venturing forth. Herbert wouldn't listen to Newton's protests that they had no time. He also dismissed Margaret's indignation about making an omelette from phoenix eggs (the rainbow eagle and phoenix were cross-breeding allies).

"We eat, therefore we are. We don't eat, we are nothing," the giant philosophized as he prepared the meal, humming an off-key tune, methodically paring and chopping as if he had all the time in the world.

To keep himself from exploding with impatience, Newton assembled his wings. By going airborne, he was certain they would cover more ground. Besides, being carried by Herbert and smelling that stench was not something he could stomach for very long.

Newton had just finished pulling the last ropes through when Herbert deposited the Phoenix-Egg Omelette in front of him. Having been absorbed in cooking, Herbert didn't notice how Newton had been occupying himself. Upon seeing the wings, he was amazed. Like the camera, for Herbert, Newton's wings were objects of great mystery and wonderment.

"Where'd you get these?" he asked, delicately fingering the membranes.

"I made them."

"Yourself? Why, they're incredible. You must be a genius!"

Newton blushed. "It's not that hard. Honest."

"How did you ever figure it out?"

"A picture of them floated into my head one day and wouldn't go away until I drew it in Journal #22. From there, I simply worked backward, disassembling the wings on paper, making a list of everything I needed. The hard part was finding all the stuff. Inventing is a lot like cooking, but with machinery instead of food."

"Have you made anything else?"

"Oh, sure. Lots of things: crystal radios, extra-strength stink bombs, solar-powered go-carts."

Herbert was flabbergasted after Newton explained what each of his inventions was. "And to think I took you for an ordinary kid. I apologize. The Merriwarts could use an inventor. How often do these pictures appear in your mind?"

"All the time. Sometimes ideas cram in so quickly that I get a headache trying to remember them. Unfortunately, most of the materials I need are either too explosive or too expensive. But when I grow up

I'm going to have my own garage where I can spend all day inventing and no one will bother me and there won't be anything I'm not allowed to do."

Herbert was still churning the idea of invention over in his mind when they sat down to eat. Much to Newton's surprise, the Phoenix-Egg Omelette, though delicious, kept re-forming itself. No sooner did he take a bite than the piece turned back into a whole again. Afraid of offending Herbert, Newton kept eating. Even when he was stuffed, it was as if he had never touched the omelette at all.

Herbert looked over at him and saw the plate. "Don't like it?" he asked suspiciously.

"No, it's—"

"It's *what?*" Herbert demanded. "No one has ever been able to resist my cooking!"

Newton was about to explain when Herbert let out a great laugh. "Just kidding. I saw you." Then Herbert told him all about how Phoenix-Egg Omelettes were known for their ability to continually re-form. "A great dish if you're having a crowd over. Remind me to give you the recipe," Herbert said, then burped.

Newton ducked but wasn't quick enough to escape the wave of foulness.

* * *

"Well, I guess Joe isn't coming back," Newton said reluctantly after doing yet another search of the cave and bushes and still not finding his friend. All along, he had secretly kept expecting Joe to turn up at any moment. Joe was famous for getting himself out of the most precarious pickles. His disappearance was worrisomely unusual.

Newton had absolutely no idea what had happened to him, but knew if they were to have any chance of stopping the wedding between Prince Natas and Princess Gertrude, they couldn't stick around any longer.

Still, leaving his friend behind was one of the hardest decisions Newton had ever made.

"I'm sure he'll turn up eventually," Herbert said when he noticed how sad Newton was.

"Maybe," Newton replied, and pinned the note he had written to Joe on the cave entrance. It explained (in code) where they had gone.

Airborne, Newton had no trouble keeping up with Herbert, and Margaret demonstrated some clever flying maneuvers that dramatically increased Newton's efficiency. He was such a quick learner that Margaret even showed him how to do the QED Double Reverse Back Flip. If you've ever seen a rainbow eagle or ten-year-old boy perform it, you know that the stunt has an extremely high degree of difficulty. After a couple of tries Newton managed awkwardly to pull it off. Though Margaret cawed with delight at her pupil's success, the effort left Newton so dizzy that he decided it was safer to stick to flying.

It didn't take them long to arrive at their destination—a dust-blown clearing surrounded by bushes. Newton landed (heels skidding to a perfect stop) while Herbert scanned the area anxiously. There were no signs of recent habitation and the clearing appeared to be deserted.

"She should be here. I don't understand," Herbert mumbled before calling out tentatively, "Grandmother Rose? Grandmother Rose? Where are you? It's me, Herbert."

But no one answered.

Anxiously, the giant got on his hands and knees and started sniffing the ground, his nose right in the dirt. When that didn't turn up any results he flicked his tongue out and licked, grinding grime in his molars in a way that made Newton shiver. After trying various dirt samples, Herbert concluded, "I don't know, maybe Rose is dead—"

A voice sounded from the bushes. "I'm not dead, just a little short of breath." Then an ancient woman appeared. She had more folds than origami and was—

Naked.

Newton, who had never seen a naked woman, much less a giant naked woman, was shocked. For the first time in his young life, he understood why people wore clothes. To be polite, Newton pretended to become very interested in his shoes.

Herbert rushed over and threw his jacket around Rose. "What has gotten into you, Grandmother Rose?" Herbert demanded.

"Oh, Herbert, don't be such a sissy. Clothes are just so . . . what's the word I'm looking for . . . ridiculous!" she replied, and tried to remove the coat, but Herbert hugged her to keep it on. "I never knew you felt this way!" Rose declared gleefully, trying to kiss Herbert, just for fun.

"Grandmother Rose, children are present!"

The ancient woman turned and looked at Newton. "Ah," she said, "the great Newton Wiggins. Witch Hazel warned me I might be getting a visit from you soon. Where's the map? Quick! Quick! You're behind schedule! Let go of me, Herbert!"

Newton reached into his knapsack and pulled out

the map, then handed it to her. Rose unrolled the parchment on the ground and knelt down for a closer examination, at one point even suspiciously putting an ear against the edges, listening for something. Newton peered over her shoulder, but the map was still blank. "Just as I feared," Rose concluded. "The map's batteries need recharging. Stand back, fellows, this might get a little dicey."

Lifting her arms in the air, Rose began chanting deep-throated, unrecognizable incantations. The sky turned black, the wind picked up, and suddenly spirits, ghosts, goblins and ghouls appeared swirling overhead, a babble of noise and motion. Some even flew through Newton (a most spine-tingling experience) before becoming caught in the frenzy. More and more circled until there was a mini-tornado of apparitions. When it seemed that they would explode from the centrifugal force, Rose brought her arms down and touched the map with her index finger. Miraculously the creatures were soaked up by the parchment like water into a sponge.

The sun once again reasserted itself and, to Newton's amazement, the map was now alive with activity. Portals popped up everywhere. "How'd you do that?" he asked, thinking Witch Hazel might be impressed with such a trick.

"A little black magic," Rose replied. "Nothing too taxing for a pro like me. I'd teach you the basics if there was more time. Maybe if you're ever in these parts again—"

"Forget it, Newton. Black magic was what got Rose kicked out of the kingdom in the first place," Herbert interrupted knowingly.

"What's the big deal? I mistakenly made the sun disappear for a whole year. Remember how much fun you had playing in the snow?"

Herbert looked mortified. "Well . . . yes. But the kingdom was forced into hibernation. No birthday parties, no games, no food, no fun, no nothing."

Rose snorted. "An unfortunate mistake during step twenty-two of the Curse of Lunar Clarity that I easily could have corrected if the elders hadn't been so quick to banish me. I yinged when I should have yanged. Could have happened to anyone."

"But you had already been given a final warning not to practice magic."

"Oh, Herbert, Herbert," Rose said, shaking her head. "We're all warned not to do *something*, aren't we? And sometimes we forget to listen. Or sometimes we don't feel like listening, or the rules are ridiculous in the first place and should be broken." Rose paused, then added, "Maybe that's what you were thinking when you decided to cook your Meal of Seduction."

Herbert blushed an embarrassed shade of deep green.

"Surprised I heard about that, huh? What you did is in the wind, Herbert. It's in our blood. So don't tell me what's what." Rose smiled mischievously before returning to the map.

"You are here," she said, pointing to an X, then ran her finger to a spot marked Y, "the Liveds' kingdom is here. The portal that will transport you there is right" —she turned and behind them was a shimmering portal— "there." It rose from the ground and gaped open like a mouth, beckoning them to step inside.

Newton and Herbert stared at it, unable to move. The map portal looked menacing. Newton was afraid if he stepped inside, he might never return. It seemed ominous, threatening.

"Well . . . ?" Rose asked impatiently. "If the Merriwarts are going to be saved, you'd better be off." She rolled up the map, handed it to Newton and started pushing them backward toward the entrance.

She stopped.

"Before you go, a warning: Whatever you do, don't lose the map. It's your key out of the Kingdom of the Liveds. Without it, you will be lost for eternity. Remember that and there's a chance you might survive. Oh, and one more thing—the bird stays. I could use a little company."

Margaret flew from Herbert's shoulder and nestled in Rose's wild hair without the least bit of hesitation or concern for loyalty.

"But—" Herbert protested.

"Don't worry. I'll take care of your precious rainbow eagle. She won't be much use to you in the land of the Liveds. Trust me, she's much safer here. Now be off. And please, don't forget about the map. Guard it with your life."

She pushed them the rest of the way in. As the portal was about to close, Rose tossed Herbert his jacket. "This stinks worse than troll poo. You might want to work on your hygiene, mister. First impressions are so important. Take my advice, Gertrude might like you a little better if you weren't such a slob."

Herbert was about to defend his sanitary habits and say something clever—like, that at least he had clothes—but the portal door shut before he could speak. Besides, Rose had already turned to walk away.

The last thing Newton saw of the giantess was her sagging rear end.

They exited the portal almost instantaneously (the best feature of portal travel for those on a tight schedule) to the most inhospitable place Newton had ever been. It made the Land of the Boulders look like a paradise. The landscape was flat, without a hill, rise or bump as far as the eye could see, except for thousands of black, burned stumps. Newton tried to swallow, but his throat was dry and his skin started itching from the lack of moisture. Newton saw huge welts erupting all over Herbert's neck and suspected his back was the same. The sky was dark gray, a low-lying haze of smog blocking out most of the sunlight.

The ground was covered with a black layer of soot that floated up and clung to their shoes and pants with each step.

Herbert's mouth hung open, and surely would have been drooling in amazement if the air weren't so dry. He bent down and ran his hand across a stump. "The Liveds told us their kingdom was a paradise," he croaked sadly. "What are these things?"

Newton, who felt as if he had laryngitis, whispered, "Stumps from trees that have been cut down. Which would explain why the Liveds are so anxious to have your forest. They've used up all their wood."

"And this . . . ?" Herbert asked, sifting ashes through his fingers.

"Ashes—what's left over after trees burn."

"Death is everywhere," Herbert said sadly, and started shaking uncontrollably. "Look at all this destruction. Who would have guessed Liveds hunted trees? Murdered them for fuel. That they didn't use lava rocks like Merriwarts do. They're barbarians."

In his rage, Herbert stomped and shouted (or tried to) and kicked up so much ash that the wind started to swirl. Soon it was impossible to see anything. Powder was everywhere. Newton covered his face with his wings, but still soot wormed its way into his eyes and ears and his airways became more and more clogged.

Newton was on the verge of suffocating, when suddenly rain fell in heavy torrents, quickly bringing the ashes back to earth and relieving his parched throat. The cloudburst lasted barely a minute, and when it had passed Newton felt as if he had eaten the contents of an ashtray.

Not surprisingly, Herbert was a wreck. He was still in shock from the stumps—and now his underwear was clammy. Foaming with worry and near hysteria (and perhaps another round of tears), Herbert turned and began walking toward the portal.

"Hey, where are you going?" Newton asked.

"It's obvious. This is bigger than us. We must leave at once. We'll go back and tell the others and get help."

Newton, sounding calmer than he felt, tried to reason with Herbert. "Please don't take this the wrong way, but your reputation is mud. Trust me, we're sunk without proof." Because Newton had spent a lifetime unsuccessfully trying to convince his parents of his brothers' evil ways, he had some expertise on the subject.

"Easy for you to say—you're brave. For cowards like me, it's much more difficult."

Newton looked at Herbert to see if he was joking. "Brave? The only reason I'm here is that I'm so scared of my brothers that I was hoping you could scare them into leaving me alone."

Herbert was loudly sucking air in and out of his nostrils. Froth had formed at the corners of his mouth.

"Listen, Herbert, you're not a coward." Newton tried to soothe him. "I just know it. To tell you the truth, I'm more than a little scared myself. I quit baseball because I was scared of getting hit by the ball. I still love getting hugs from Max's mom. So don't get the wrong idea that I'm any braver. Trust me, you'll always regret it if you back out now."

"At least I'll still be alive to have regret," Herbert shot back. He took a deep breath, and for a moment Newton thought he was wavering. But then he asked, "Won't you come with me?"

Newton shook his head. "No. I'm going to see this through. I've come too far and I'd feel awful if I gave up now."

"But what's in it for you? Why do you care about us Merriwarts?"

A fair question, but one that Newton didn't have an answer to. "I don't know. It just feels like the thing I should be doing. I can't explain it any better than that. If I get through this, maybe other things in my life will be easier. Then again, maybe they won't, but I'll never know unless I try."

Herbert had no idea what Newton was talking

about. The sky thundered. “I’ve got to go,” he declared sadly, then walked into the portal and disappeared.

As simple as that.

First Max. Then Commander Joe. Now Herbert. Everyone kept abandoning Newton. Maybe people just didn’t like him.

He took out the portal map and tried to find the entrance to the Kingdom of the Liveds that Rose had shown him. Without Herbert around, Newton didn’t feel nearly so adventurous. He told himself not to look back and double-check to see if Herbert was following. The giant had made his decision, and that was that. There was no use straining his neck to confirm the obvious. But flying over the ash-soaked ground, Newton couldn’t hold his resolve, and every few seconds he turned, desperately hoping Herbert had had a change of heart.

Of course he hadn’t. The landscape was completely Merriwart-free as Newton continued his lonely flight.

Chapter 11

Staring at the entrance to the Lived lair—a door made of solid rock without handles or hinges that seemed as immovable as a mountain—Newton hoped he had arrived at the wrong destination. Rechecking the map only confirmed this was the place. The door would not budge, no matter how hard he pushed, pulled and pried—not even a micrometer. A search for a hidden lever revealed nothing, and chanting a number of popular secret passwords proved equally fruitless.

However, in spite of his complete failure to make any inroads, Newton was not wholly discouraged.

The entrance seemed familiar. He had read about entrances like this before. But where? Instinctively he was certain that if he could remember, he would be able to unlock the secret. His mind was buzzing with codes and combinations. He held his head very still, so his thoughts wouldn't become jumbled, and tried to think.

He rubbed his temples. He scrunched up his eyes. He pulled his earlobes. He wished Joe (with his vast experience sneaking behind enemy lines) were around to help him out. He wiggled his toes. He made chirping sounds. All of the usual tricks to shake up his gray matter. But still Newton was flummoxed and the first traces of panic (increased heart rate and clammy feet) started to make their presence felt.

Then the solution came to him in a flash. Newton remembered! Of course! How could he have missed it! This must be the famous Houdini Door (which he had read all about in book number 232 of the Detective Pinewood series, *Houdini Enters*). It had to be, he was certain—if he pressed his nose against the door he could just barely see the crossed lines. The only trick was remembering the rules of engagement—a slip of protocol would be utterly disastrous.

Therefore, Newton would be extra, extra careful.

He bent down and picked up a handful of ash, then rubbed it in circles on the middle of the door. As he rubbed, slowly there emerged a tic-tac-toe board, the game already in progress.

The door had marked an X in the upper left corner, so Newton countered with an O in the center. The door came back with an X in the lower right corner and Newton placed an O in the upper right corner.

The moment of truth had arrived.

Everything hung on the door's next move.

An X appeared in the lower left corner.

Newton knew that the door was now in a winning position two different ways. The game was over. Newton drew an O in the middle left box. Immediately the door produced an X in the middle of the lower row.

Newton had lost!

He took two steps back and waited expectantly. The door remained motionless. For a moment Newton panicked that he had somehow offended it. But to his huge relief, the stone slab slowly, silently began to slide open.

Newton knew, of course, that the secret to a Houdini Door is letting the door win without making it obvious—a strategy remarkably similar to playing checkers with a five-year-old. You had to try hard to look like you really wanted to win so as not to arouse suspicion. But if you went for the kill and won, well, there'd be tears.

The entrance led directly to a tunnel. Newton, camera slung around his neck, still wearing his wings, began walking. The walls were moist and the only light came from the floor that glowed a murky red. Newton crouched down and tried to figure out the source of the light, but couldn't tell if the glow came from the rocks or a gel-like substance between them. Cursing that he hadn't packed his *Field Guide to Extraterrestrial Rock Samples*, Newton snapped a picture of the floor for identification purposes later.

The map clearly indicated that the route to the heart of the Lived lair lay straight ahead. As Newton continued to creep ever deeper into the tunnel, he wondered when he would encounter his first Lived and what kind of mood he or she would be in. But the place was eerily deserted. Where was everyone? Did they have unseen monitors tracking his every

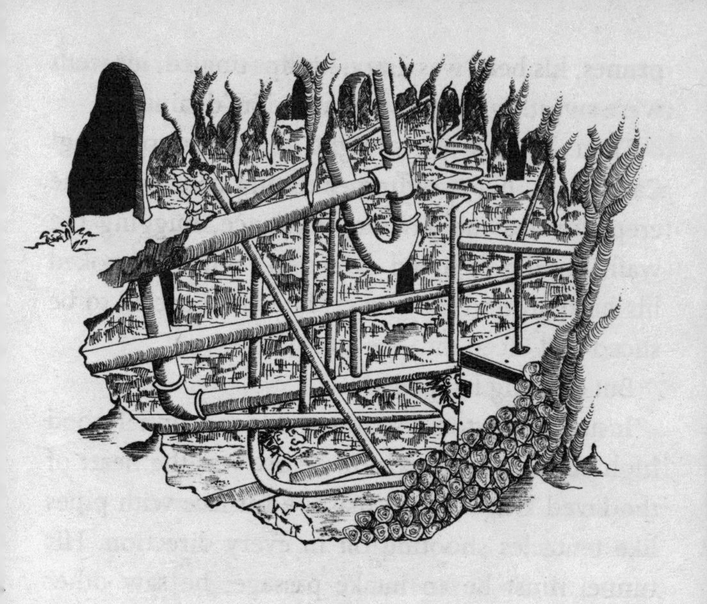

move? Newton was straining so much to hear through the silence, his eardrums were practically screaming. Something definitely didn't feel right—his heebie-jeebie sensors told him to turn and run away as fast as he could. But Newton continued walking. Twice he popped his ears to equalize the pressure buildup from the descent.

Aside from the occasional fork in the tunnel, the only change in his surroundings was a steady increase in temperature. Soon the heat was approaching unbearable. Newton's hands were prunes, his head was dizzy, his lips tingled, his teeth were sweating, and he was afraid he'd faint.

Then he saw it—straight ahead: an opening! Cautiously, like a swimmer testing cold water, he crept toward the yawning entrance, hugging the wall, hoping to avoid detection. When he poked his head around the corner, he half expected to be sliced and diced into the afterworld.

But nothing happened.

Instead, Newton discovered that the tunnel stood high above a huge cavern. Below was the heart of the Lived kingdom—a massive furnace with pipes like tentacles shooting off in every direction. His tunnel must be an intake passage; he saw other similar openings around the cavern. The air was thick (most likely with some kind of toxic by-product of the burning) and enormous piles of logs reached up and touched the stalactites dripping from the ceiling. Four Liveds were carting logs to the furnace, continually stoking the fire. They went about their business without much enthusiasm, hanging their heads, shuffling their feet. Newton looked around, convinced there had to be more Liveds. However, unless they were playing an extremely long game of hide-and-seek, he couldn't see any.

Wiping the sweat from his eyes, Newton held up his camera and took three pictures—one of the furnace, one of the logs and the last of the Liveds at work. Even the flash didn't distract the Liveds from their drudgery.

Newton had his proof of the Liveds' dastardly ways! Once the Merriwarts saw the photos, they would never agree to become allies with the Liveds. Carefully Newton tucked the pictures in his front pocket and fastened the button to prevent them from falling out.

At this point Newton should have turned around and skedaddled out of there as fast as his overheated legs and wings would carry him—especially in light of the fact that Gertrude was to be married in mere hours. Besides, who knows the long-term lung damage caused by breathing in such putrid cave air. But for someone so smart, Newton, on occasion, was incredibly stupid.

Unfortunately this was one of those occasions.

Curiosity ate at him like rust through metal. Why had the Liveds destroyed their kingdom to feed the fire? Something sinister *had* to be behind their actions. A nuclear reactor? A science experiment? Were they melting metal into gold? Looking for the secret to the universe?

Then Newton saw what he was certain was the key to unlocking the mystery. Beside the furnace was a black box, no bigger than a coffin. A sixth sense (which may or may not have been fully functioning) convinced him that whatever was inside it would answer every question he had ever had . . . about anything. He tucked the portal map in his back pocket.

So Newton did the unthinkable, the exact opposite of mission protocol—he set out toward the black box. After fluttering up to an overhead pipe, he began walking toward the biggest pile of logs in the center of the cavern. (He would have flown down, but figured walking was the best way to avoid detection.) As he inched his way along, Newton kept expecting the Liveds to see him, but they never looked up, continuing their work without pause. It was only a short hop off the pipe to the log pile, where Newton scrambled down until the only thing separating him from the black box was a few feet of sooty floor. And, of course, four Liveds.

But the drones seemed entirely uninterested in anything other than their endless shuffle from log pile to furnace.

This was going to be so easy.

•

The exact moment that all four Liveds were turned the other way, Newton dashed toward the black box and dove behind it for cover. He took a couple of seconds to calm down before cautiously placing a trembling hand on the lid. If the black box contained the formula for life, he would be the first kid ever to win a Nobel Prize!

Newton saw that the Liveds still had their backs turned to him. It was now or never. He took a deep breath and flipped up the lid. As soon as Newton opened it, he knew he had made a colossal mistake.

A terrifying howl came from the box and before he could slam shut the lid, out leaped the strangest creature Newton had ever seen. Newton recognized it from his *Field Guide to Scary Creatures* as a Tasmanian Troll. The whirling dervish flailed with the fury of a frog in a blender, then flew out of the room, howling with delight at his unexpected freedom, long gone before anyone could make a move to recapture him.

This was not exactly the life-changing universal secret Newton had anticipated unearthing.

The Liveds stared, open mouthed, at Newton, drool pooling at their feet. *Lunch had escaped!* For creatures who had absolutely nothing else in their dreary days to look forward to, losing a meal was unthinkable, inexcusable and completely intolerable.

In the troll's place stood Newton, who was about the same size and looked considerably less hairy and much more succulent. The four Liveds dropped their logs and advanced toward Newton with grumbling stomachs. Newton realized that they were looking at him as their lunch—an entirely unnerving experience.

Quickly scanning the cave, Newton looked for an escape route. Wood piles surrounded him on two sides, the Liveds on the third and the furnace blocked the fourth. If he had any chance of avoiding capture, up was the only way to go. However, the Liveds were too close for him to take off. As they advanced closer, Newton felt the air grow colder. The creatures were a solid wall pressing in, about to trap him. At the last moment, Newton saw his chance. Head-faking left, he shot through an opening between the legs of the middle Lived. A fraction of a second slower and Newton would have had his skull crushed by knees slamming shut the gap.

Instead, the chase was on. Newton, now in frantic pre-flight mode, began flapping, hoping to reach one of the tunnel entrances surrounding the cavern. He rose quickly in the heat and felt the brush of fingertips against his ankle, but dared not look down.

The Liveds, energized by the threat of losing lunch, were now moving much more quickly, cutting off Newton's escape routes as fast as he could plan them. For bulky creatures they could leap like kangaroos right up to the tunnel entrances high above.

The effort of flapping and the intolerable heat were making Newton's head feel like it would explode and his heart go *boom-boom-boom* at an alarming rate. The tunnel on the opposite side of the cavern was only a few flaps away, but a Lived had seen where Newton was headed and got there first, blocking the entrance. Newton tilted his wings and veered sharply, trying to reach the next entrance over. No sooner had he done this than he saw another Lived in his path. His vision blurred by sweat, Newton dipped his left wing so that it almost touched his foot, just to avoid being plucked out of the air (almost stalling himself in the process). How did the Liveds manage to be everywhere at once?

Newton's body temperature continued to rise. He was now a wounded bird, and the Liveds grunted in anticipation as they moved in for the kill. Exhausted, Newton summoned all his energy and flapped to the top of the cavern. With his sights set on a nearby tunnel, he tucked in his wings and nose-dived toward it, knowing this was his last hope. The tactic dramatically increased his speed (though Newton feared if he actually made it to the tunnel, the crash-landing might kill him).

The Liveds, caught off guard, scrambled to reach the entrance in time. For a moment they appeared to be too late, but then one flew from the pile and plucked Newton out of the air like a wide receiver catching a football.

The other Liveds rushed over and grabbed him. In spite of the inferno of the cavern, immediately Newton was freezing—all warmth sucked out of him. To be touched by the Liveds felt like being dunked in a vat of slush. He shivered and his teeth chattered and his head hurt as if he had eaten a gallon of ice cream without stopping.

Newton cursed his stupidity. What had he been thinking? Why hadn't he simply turned and gone back through the tunnel? Certain some horrible, life-ending fate awaited, Newton was helpless as the Liveds marched him back toward the black box.

Distracted by the Liveds' pinching, prodding and

roughhousing, Newton never felt the portal map fall out of his back pocket and land silently on the ground.

The group stopped in front of the black box. "Should we chop him up now?" one of the Liveds asked. The voice was deep-throated and produced a wet noise that made Newton shiver even more. How he wished they'd let him go so he could warm up again. His bones ached from the cold.

"Naw. We'll hair-boil him later. That way he'll be much fresher," another answered.

"Then you get the head," the third joked.

Newton couldn't understand why they all thought this was hilarious. Hearing the Liveds' laughter had the same effect on Newton as chewing tinfoil.

The fourth, with wild red hair and pudgy hands (who squeezed Newton's left ankle too tightly), asked, "Grunt, grunt, grunt?" then looked at Newton questioningly.

Newton, who spoke not a word of Grunt-ese, squeaked out, "What did you say?"

"Who are you?" Red replied. "What are you doing here? Why did you release our lunch? How much do you weigh?"

"Newton Wiggins. I'm lost. It was an accident. Sixty-four and three-quarter pounds," Newton answered, recalling that his *Ten Ways to Talk to Your Torturers* manual strongly suggested brevity as the route to survival. Red ripped the camera from around Newton's neck and pulverized it into nothingness with his foot.

"*LIAR!*" he shouted, then tore off Newton's wings and tossed them into the furnace. They melted instantly. "Who sent you?"

How Newton wished the Liveds would stop shouting. Their yelling felt like a dentist's drill boring through his front teeth. The pain was so overwhelming, Newton didn't even care about the wings. "I entered a wrong portal and ended up in a tunnel," he said quickly.

This was not the answer the Liveds were looking for. They roared and started pulling at his limbs, each yanking in a different direction. "Tell us or die!" But Newton could not speak through the pain. He knew that his life was over and hoped that they would finish him off quickly because he didn't want to give them the satisfaction of watching him blubber like a baby.

Then, seemingly from out of nowhere, came another howl. Newton couldn't see what it was, but the Liveds dropped Newton to deal with this new threat.

Newton couldn't believe he was free. He rolled over, looked between the Liveds' legs and saw a wonderful sight! Herbert was rushing straight toward the Liveds. They were lined up shoulder to shoulder, like four soccer players blocking a penalty kick, bracing themselves to meet the challenge. Herbert came at them roaring furiously, spit and gunk spewing out of his mouth.

As he approached them he appeared to speed up. For their part, the Liveds looked less sure the closer Herbert came. They tried to make eye contact, they puffed their chests, they even roared their most fearsome roars, but still he came.

Herbert wasn't even looking at the Liveds, but beyond them to Newton. The heat seemed to energize the giant. He looked powerful, like he might be able to chew bricks for breakfast and spit them out at lunch. Less than six strides separated him from his goal.

Herbert was a blur, and in unison the Liveds began reciting, "*Hit the enemy where it hurts! Hit the enemy when their backs are turned! Hit the enemy below the belt!*"

At the moment before impact, three of the four Liveds jumped out of the way.

The runaway Merriwart crashed through the

courageous (but ultimately stupid) Lived like a hockey puck through wet toilet paper, knocking him out cold. Herbert never broke stride but scooped up Newton and sprinted onto the log pile. The three remaining Liveds took up the chase, determined not to let the invaders escape.

The Liveds were even quicker than Herbert. By the time they reached the top of the log pile, Herbert's lead had been erased like chalk off a blackboard.

"They're close!" Newton yelled. "Hurry!"

"How close?" Herbert gasped.

"Three yards."

Herbert stopped instantly. With his free hand (he dared not let go of Newton), Herbert scooped up a medium-size log and hurled it at the Liveds. *Strike!* The log caught one directly between the eyes. As he crumpled to the ground, he knocked his partners over.

Herbert kept running.

The two Liveds rose up again, further enraged. They came after Herbert with a renewed vengeance.

Only steps away from the top of the pile, Herbert increased his efforts, ignoring his burning legs and heaving lungs. "You can make it!" Newton urged, confident Herbert could easily jump the gap between the pile and the tunnel entrance.

And he would have, if the accident hadn't happened.

As Herbert was set to leap off the log pile, he tripped. A silly blunder, but altogether excusable. (Newton later learned that his shoelace had come undone a few days before and Herbert never had found the time or interest to retie it, not surprising considering he didn't often wear shoes.)

Fortunately, when Herbert fell, he avoided landing on Newton and squishing him like a ripe banana.

Still holding Newton, Herbert wasted no time in scrambling to his feet. But the Liveds were too quick and they jumped on Herbert, clinging to his back like metal filings to a magnet.

"Let me go, Herbert!" Newton shouted, knowing the situation was dire and that Herbert would be better off fighting with two free hands. Newton also had a plan. Not much of one, but under the circumstances it was amazing he could think of anything at all.

However, Herbert still held onto him as the Liveds pounded his back and pulled his hair in a desperate attempt to bring him down again.

"Herbert, now! Let go!"

Staggering, Herbert had no choice. He dropped Newton.

"*Argggh!!*" Herbert screamed when a Lived bit into his neck.

As soon as Newton hit the ground, he scurried between Herbert's feet and quickly tied together his shoelaces, afraid that if he lingered too long, Herbert might accidentally walk on him.

"Herbert, run backward!" Newton ordered, once he had cleared out of the way.

The Liveds were still on his back. Both were biting into him. Herbert didn't question the order but did as he was told.

The giant staggered for a couple of steps, trying to keep his balance, but because his shoelaces were tied together, he toppled over.

The fall surely would have broken his spine except that the Liveds were underneath to cushion his landing. Newton heard the horrifying *squish!* and was certain the Liveds had ruptured a few organs (not their hearts, though—those were too cold, too unfeeling to be damaged). They lay motionless.

Newton untied Herbert's shoelaces. The giant was still lying on top of them, dazed. "What happened?" he asked, looking around.

"You saved the day," Newton said. "Let's go!"

Herbert got up and grabbed Newton and ran. The distance to the tunnel entrance looked too far. If they missed, well . . .

"Jump, Herbert! You can do it!"

Herbert took a deep breath, bent his knees and leaped toward the tunnel.

Newton closed his eyes, afraid that if Herbert somehow miscalculated the distance from the top of the woodpile to the entrance . . . well, Newton didn't want to think about that.

Newton landed with a *thud* and opened his eyes, looking around in amazement.

"You made it, Herbert!" Newton shouted.

"So I did," Herbert gasped, "so I did."

Fearing that the Liveds might come after them at any moment, Newton wasted no more time appreciating Herbert's athletic feat and urged the giant on, though he could see that Herbert was very, very tired. But Herbert picked Newton up and began running.

They ran down the tunnel and started turning right and then left, winding their way blindly through the maze, their only thought to elude their foes.

After they had covered what seemed like a marathon distance, Herbert stopped.

They noticed that the tunnel had cooled off. There was no sight or sound of the Liveds, and they were sure they had put enough distance between them.

All at once, in a rush, fatigue caught up with Herbert. Bent over, grabbing his knees, the giant panted with exhaustion—his chest heaving, his legs twitching.

It took a few minutes of recovering before Herbert finally was able to spit out the details of his desertion-reversal decision. As soon as the giant had abandoned Newton, a number of different emotions had swirled around his big-little brain. Oh sure, he huffed and he puffed about the hopelessness of their mission, about the direness of the situation, about how he had done the smart thing by leaving. But really, underneath it all, Herbert was scared, homesick and, truth be told, slightly in awe of Newton. The kid was heroic.

Once he realized why he had left, that his reasons for deserting Newton were lies, he turned around. However, finding Newton again proved more than a little complicated. Twice he had made wrong turns. At the Houdini Door Herbert stubbornly had refused to let the entrance win at tic-tac-toe until the twenty-fifth game.

As a result, Herbert finally found Newton right when the Liveds were about to rip him into pieces and eat him raw like sushi.

"Herbert, I don't know how to thank you. I thought—" Newton began, but the giant weakly raised a hand. Both knew it would be better to leave certain things unsaid. But Newton couldn't help adding, "Herbert, saving me was the bravest thing I've ever seen."

Herbert blushed about eight shades of green. "Really?" he finally asked, looking up.

"Absolutely," Newton assured him.

Herbert sniffled, then continued catching his breath.

All that remained was to return to the Kingdom of the Merriwarts and find out if they were in time to prevent a wedding.

Newton reached into his back pocket to bring out the map. It was then that he discovered the map was gone. He searched, re-searched and turned out every pocket, but of course it didn't turn up.

He looked at Herbert in horror. The one thing he wasn't supposed to lose was lost. Even if they managed to make it out of the Lived lair, without the map it would be almost impossible to locate the portal again.

Chapter 12

Newton looked at his watch. In less than two hours Gertrude's bachelorette days would be over and she'd be Mrs. Lived—married to the enemy. Neither Newton nor Herbert knew what to do next. Still, things could have been slightly worse—at least they were still alive to know they were in deep, deep trouble.

Unable to devise a better plan of escape, they started walking through the Lived tunnels (actually, Newton jogged), hoping to stumble upon the Houdini Door. In spite of Newton's best efforts to stay brave, fears of a lifetime spent wandering this maze, of never finding his way out and of starving to death, crept over him, tickling his neck hairs and making his knees wobbly.

They walked.

And they walked. Right. Left. Up. Down. Newton had no idea which way they were going. Several times Newton was sure he heard a faint honking sound, but when he turned around, he couldn't see anything.

Finally, in the middle of a tunnel, Newton stopped abruptly (almost causing Herbert to trample him) and turned to look over his shoulder.

He saw it—something white and thin, floating off the ground, advancing toward them like a magic carpet. Would it maliciously speed up and slice their heads off?

The object halted at their feet, but Newton still could not make it out in the gloom, though it looked familiar. A newspaper? A book? A towel?

"What is it?" Herbert whispered.

"I'm not sure," Newton replied. They backed up, but the object followed, again stopping in front of them, as if it were attached to them by a string.

Herbert raised a leg. "I'll stomp it a few times to be safe."

But Newton suddenly knew exactly what the

object was and scurried under Herbert's massive foot. "Stop! It's the portal map!" he shouted, and stretched out his hand to snatch it from the air.

"Be careful, Newton," Herbert warned. "Why would the portal map be following us? I'm absolutely positive it's been rigged. Maybe poisoned by the Liveds. Trust me, I can sniff out a trap from two kingdoms away."

Newton hesitated. Ever since the embarrassing time his brothers had fooled him into believing he had won the Boy of the Year Award (obviously no such award exists, but when you're three, it's hard to know better), he had hated being tricked. But this seemed too advanced for the Liveds. "Maybe you've got a stuffed nose and your sniffer isn't working properly, but this is definitely the portal map. Besides, what do we have to lose?"

Herbert said he would ignore the nose comment and that he realized Newton had a point. They were up to their eyeballs in trouble. So what if they sunk farther into it?

Newton grabbed the portal map and braced himself for the possibility of being blown to smithereens.

The paper didn't explode. Limbs didn't melt. Poison gas didn't suffocate them.

Instead, as soon as Newton lifted the parchment, who should appear from underneath it but . . .

"*Commander Joe!*" Newton shouted. There he was, Newton's pint-size pal, driving a miniature Jeep. Which would explain the honking he had thought he'd heard earlier. Beside him, riding shotgun in the passenger seat, sat a woman the same size as Joe, wearing a white lab coat and black horn-rimmed glasses. Masking tape held the glasses together at the nose.

Newton peppered Joe with question after question, never bothering to wait for an answer. Where had Joe disappeared to? How did he manage to find him? Where did he get the portal map? Who was the mystery woman? How did the Jeep fly in the air?

"Relax. Manners, soldier. Questions need answers and answers take time and that's something we're seriously short of at the moment. For now, may I proudly introduce none other than the universally famous scientist, Dr. Birdy Doosler, head of the Intergalactic Patent Office."

Dr. Doosler stood up, held onto the roll bar and extended her delicate hand toward Newton. "A pleasure to finally meet you."

Newton was confused. *Finally meet him?* How did a stranger know who he was?

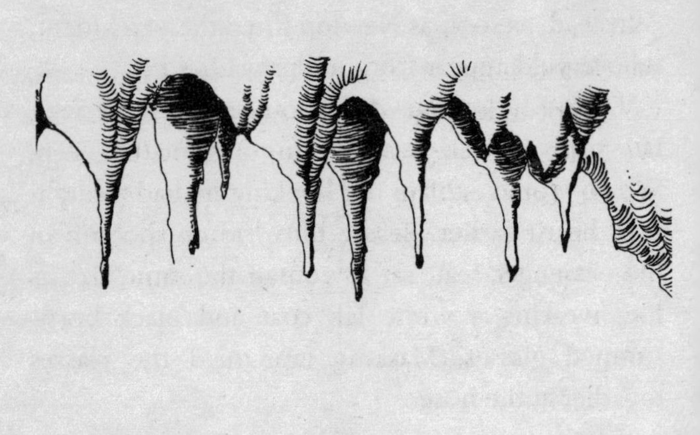

"Time's wasting, people," Joe declared. "If there's any hope of saving this big oaf's kingdom, we've got to move out now. Herbert, pick us up. We'll ride on your shoulders and I'll direct you out of here. Let's go!"

In a matter of moments, Newton had gone from feeling lower than an octopus at the bottom of the ocean to having all the hope in the world. Between barking directions at Herbert, Joe recounted to Newton the strange tale of his adventures.

The last time Newton had seen Joe, the action figure had been about to enter Herbert's cave. But as Joe reached the entrance, he spied something slithering in the bushes. It looked like the same thing he'd caught out of the corner of his eye when he and Newton had slid under the home plate portal. After faking as if he were entering the cave, Joe snuck up on Dr. Doosler. Dr. Doosler was so surprised that she zapped them both back to the MacArthur Universal Inventions Headquarters located in southern Jupiter.

"I got sidetracked, so to speak. Sorry for the delay, Pokey."

"But, why? What was Dr. Doosler doing?" Newton asked.

"Dr. Doosler can speak for herself," Dr. Doosler

interjected. "Our company has been monitoring your invention work, Newton. We're impressed. Your flying machine is a work of genius. I was sent to offer you a deal—to buy the Universal Patent Rights. But first, I had to make sure the wings worked. Of course, in the process, I was the one who dislodged the pin in the Land of the Boulders. An honest mistake and I sincerely hope you will accept my apologies for nearly killing you."

Newton accepted her apologies and was glad finally to have an explanation for the loose pin—he would hate to get a reputation as an absentminded inventor. Secretly Newton was also extremely proud that his work had caught the attention of such a prestigious institution. Until he remembered that his precious invention had been tossed into the furnace.

"But my wings are burned," Newton lamented.

"Yes, about your wings being burned—" Dr. Doosler began.

"You nearly got yourself killed, mister," Joe scolded. "What were you thinking? You already had the photographs. That little stunt broke about two hundred rules of combat. If I were your commanding officer, you would be court-martialed."

"Dumb. Dumb. Dumb," Dr. Doosler added.

Newton blushed. "I just wanted to find out what was inside the black box."

Joe continued. "Because we arrived at the cavern through a different tunnel, you never saw our waving or heard our shouting. All we could do was watch in horror, concluding you were as good as lunch. Then *Wham! Bam! Kaslam!* Herbert goes kamikaze, pulls you out of the fire, so to speak, and the game is still on. When we saw the map fall out, we drove down, picked it up, tied it to the top of the Jeep and chased after you."

"About your invention going up in smoke," Dr. Doosler said reassuringly. "All we need are your schematic drawings."

Schematic drawings! Newton was about to explain how the quadruplets had stolen his journal, when Joe ordered Herbert to make a sharp left. Suddenly the Houdini Door was before them. Herbert rapped three times and it opened (Houdini Doors were far easier to exit by than to enter).

Once outside, they scanned the portal map, searching for the entrance back to the Kingdom of the Merriwarts. "Oh, no," Joe groaned. "This is catastrophic! Look, our portal's miles away! We'll never make it!"

"My kingdom is doomed!" Herbert wailed dramatically. "Alas, poor, poor me!"

"Relax, Herbert," Newton said, and turned the map around. "Try looking at it right side up. See, the portal's right there."

"And that spot must be—" Herbert began.

"Right over there!" Joe said excitedly. "Look!" He pointed to a portal that stood glowing like a lighthouse on a lonely seacoast, less than a football field away.

Joe looked at his shock-resistant field watch. Ten minutes after five! The wedding had already begun.

"Run, Herbert! Run!" Newton shouted.

Joe pulled at Herbert's ear, urging him to speed up, like a jockey on a horse. Dr. Doosler held onto Joe so he wouldn't fall out of the Jeep. Under normal circumstances Herbert would have refused to be treated in this manner. But these were not normal circumstances. Instead, Herbert put his head down and redoubled his efforts in an all-out dash to save the kingdom.

Chapter 13

They exited the portal high above the ground in a tree house belonging to Herbert's cousin Antonio. No one was home. Gulping in lungfuls of clean Merriwart air, Herbert quickly recovered. Though his legs still burned and he was soaked with sweat, he ordered everyone to hold on tightly and leaped off the ledge of Anonio's place into the air, shouting, "To the banquet hall!"

"*Herrrberrrttt!*" Joe, Dr. Doosler and Newton all shouted at once, convinced that the giant had finally snapped. Newton was so sure he was going to die that part of his life flashed before him (the preschool years), but Herbert extended his long arms and expertly caught a branch. The limb bent and groaned and seemed on the verge of snapping, then sling-shot them toward the next tree. Joe and Dr. Doosler got a mild case of whiplash (but enjoyed the roller-coaster effect immensely). Crashing through leaves, Herbert caught another branch and the same thing happened. By the tenth tree, Newton was no longer afraid and realized this was how Merriwarts traveled around their kingdom, **boink! boink! boink!** from tree to tree.

In no time they landed on the platform outside the Great Hall—the same hall where Newton had seen Prince Natas propose to Gertrude on his earlier visit.

Below, a caravan of carts circled the base of the tree. "That must be the water Prince Natas promised Princess Gertrude as a wedding gift," Herbert concluded. "I sure could use a jug."

Though Newton couldn't say what it was, something about the carts tickled his suspicious bone. Joe looked over, and Newton knew he was thinking the same thing.

There were no windows to look through, just a peephole that Herbert hogged. He peered into the banquet hall and didn't say a word.

Were they too late?

"Don't sugarcoat it, tell us the bad news. We can take it," Joe demanded.

"More importantly, what does the bride's dress look like?" Dr. Doosler asked.

Herbert squinted for a moment longer, completely distracted, before wistfully saying, "I've never seen Gertrude look so beautiful. She has just removed her shoes. Oh, what beautiful toenails!"

Joe rolled his eyes. "Listen, Romeo, focus. There's no time for love when a soldier is in mission mode. Details: Are we too late? Is the princess hitched? The suspense is making my arm socket itch," Joe said testily, and scratched the hole where his left arm once hung.

The giant continued looking through the peephole. "They're only at the Licking of the Feet part of the ceremony, which means . . . Gertrude's not married yet! Hooray!"

"It's our lucky day, lover boy," Joe barked. "Okay, tell me how many Liveds are inside and whether they're packing clubs, swords or any kind of firepower." Newton was impressed by Joe's ability to stay so focused in the field.

"I count eight," Herbert replied. "They're dressed from gill to toe in black. I don't see any weapons, though it looks like they could easily hide something underneath their robes."

Joe paced and pondered, lost in strategizing. "The Liveds are clearly outnumbered by Merriwarts," he said aloud, "which means they wouldn't dare make a move. Normally in these situations I'd call for the heavy artillery, but since we don't have any firepower, our options are limited. So here's the plan, simple and elegant: We'll go in together, show the photos and hope for the best."

Everyone agreed that this was the only course of action.

Everyone except Newton. Perhaps it was the uneasy feeling about the Lived carts parked below, but Newton did not want to enter the banquet hall with Herbert. He wanted to stay behind, just in case they needed a backup plan. Fishing the photos out of his pocket, Newton handed all but one to Herbert. "Here, take these. You don't need us. I'm sure everything will be fine, but, just in case . . ."

"Newton!" Herbert gasped. "We're a team! We've come this far together."

"I'm not changing my mind. Don't worry, I'll be right here." Since the Licking of the Feet was about to start, Herbert quickly agreed to go inside alone.

Newton secretly suspected that part of the giant was relieved he wouldn't have to share the glory.

Joe looked at Newton. "What's your plan, Pokey?"

"What do you mean?" Newton asked innocently.

"I saw you keep one of the photos. Something's going on." It was true, Newton had kept one for himself.

"Well, you're the one who taught me that a soldier always needs a backup plan."

"I did. So, what's yours?"

"Well, that's the problem," Newton admitted. "I haven't figured one out yet, but I'm working on it."

Joe started the engine to the Jeep. "While you're monitoring the situation from up here and strategizing, Dr. Doosler and I will drive down and confirm the cart contents." Without waiting for an answer, Joe peeled away at hyper-speed, leaving a strip of rubber on Newton's shoulder.

* * *

Newton ran to the window on the other side of the platform and was peering through before Herbert entered the Great Hall. Outfitted in their wedding finest (colored rags, hats with real birds nesting on top of them and shoes that seemed to have springs on them), the Merriwarts were giving each other confused looks. Then Newton saw what the problem was: Prince Natas still hadn't sucked Gertrude's

toes. He was obviously trying to psych himself up enough to finish the ceremony. But Natas looked green, like he might puke, and his eyes were watering. Newton saw Natas's brother poke him a couple of times, trying to nudge the groom into action.

The window was open and Newton could see and hear everything.

"Prince Natas, we're waiting," an elderly Merriwart said impatiently. "Is there something wrong? As you know, in order for the marriage to take place, custom demands that you must lick every crack and crease of Gertrude's wonderful toes."

"But the nails are uncut, mold's growing between her toes, and look at all those warts!" Natas complained. "Throw in the smell and these feet are, without a doubt, the most disgusting appendages I've ever seen."

The Merriwarts clapped and looked proudly at one another. "We couldn't agree more. Indeed, they are!" The elder beamed.

Natas swallowed dryly. "Well . . . yes."

At that moment, the banquet hall doors creaked open. Heads turned to see who entered.

Herbert! A collective gasp went up. *"How dare the exile return!" "Does he have no shame!" "Where is the decency!" "And on her wedding day!" "Especially during this, the most beautiful part of the ceremony!"* Newton heard various Merriwarts exclaim.

Herbert ignored the comments and, before anyone could stop him, marched to the altar and turned to face his people. For a moment he said nothing. Newton guessed he was imagining how, centuries later, historians would retell the legend of his brave deeds.

Newton silently urged Herbert to get on with it. He saw the Liveds advance menacingly toward his friend.

Luckily Herbert seemed to notice too. Holding the photographs before him like the Holy Grail—though they looked like postage stamps in the giant's hands—Herbert announced dramatically, "I HAVE COME TO SAVE OUR KINGDOM. I HAVE RETURNED TO WARN YOU THAT THE LIVEDS PLAN TO CUT DOWN EVERY LAST ONE OF OUR TREES AND BURN THEM! I HAVE PROOF! THE LIVEDS ARE—"

But Herbert did not have a chance to finish his accusations. Led by Natas—who obviously needed about as much reason to fight as the wind needs to blow—the Liveds tackled Herbert to the ground like a cement truck running over a mouse. There was a flurry of kicking, punching, biting and pulling of hair. The Merriwarts, unused to displays of violence, watched in stunned helplessness as the beating seemed to go on forever. By the time the last Lived had peeled himself off, Herbert was senseless, his nose bloody, his eyes swollen shut and his precious photos mysteriously gone.

Newton scrambled down from the window and quickly ran into the banquet hall, not sure what he was going to do but knowing he had to do something.

Herbert was still motionless. Newton was scared he was dead but refused to give the idea too much brain-time in case he started to cry.

An elder Merriwart rose and was about to say something, when Natas silenced him with a look that could pulverize stone. Straightening his tunic, then clearing his throat, Natas announced, "No need to thank us. Glad to be of assistance."

The Merriwarts looked shocked. Newton could see that Herbert, exiled or not, clearly needed help, and yet, with the Lived Royal Court glaring at them, no one would be brave enough to tend to his wounds. Instead Herbert was left on the ground, possibly dying, certainly in a great deal of pain.

A malicious smile spread across Natas's face as he turned to Gertrude. "Now, where were we? Ah, yes. I was about to have the unique pleasure of licking your feet. Then we will finally be married."

Before Gertrude could protest, Prince Natas bent over and stuck Gertrude's little toe in his mouth, making loud sucking noises as custom dictated. Newton would not have been surprised if he bit her pinky toe right off. Twice Natas gagged but faked a cough.

Unnoticed, Newton nudged a giantess and handed her his last photo, knowing that if she didn't take the bait or decide to eat him, the game was over. Luckily the giantess simply put the photo right in front of her face, squinched her eyes and saw the picture of murdered trees and Liveds in their lair.

Newton saw that the Merriwart instantly understood the thousand-word story the picture had to tell—in spite of its size. She nudged her seatmate hard in the ribs and passed the photo on. Quickly, like a hot potato, the photo traveled from Merriwart to Merriwart.

And with it dawned the realization that Herbert had been telling the truth! The mood in the banquet hall slowly changed from shock to outright horror.

The Liveds were liars!

Here was the proof!

Meanwhile, Prince Natas flicked his tongue out. He had finished with Gertrude's toes, and all that separated them from becoming husband and wife was one last sole. Perhaps imagining how wonderfully the Merriwart forest would burn, how the fire from the logs would warm his icy blood for many æons, he took a deep breath and licked.

The Royal Court, absorbed in watching Natas, didn't notice Newton as he walked over to Herbert and opened his eyelids. The eyes were lifeless and unfocused. A small stream of blood trickled out of his left ear and was quickly soaked up by the dirt floor. Newton grabbed Herbert's wrist and searched for a pulse, but could feel nothing.

Herbert was dead.

The giant had been slayed! Unable to control himself, Newton let out a yell that came from deep within him—a cry that released a lifetime of unfairness. His anguish and anger rebounded off the walls and exploded.

Silence.

The Merriwarts froze.

The Liveds froze.

Herbert remained motionless.

Prince Natas, wavering between finishing the

licking ceremony or discovering the fool who had dared interrupt him, lifted his head. He was incredulous to see, standing on the fallen giant's chest, a creature no bigger than lunch. Natas rose, towering over Newton like a storm. His eyes smoldered, and Newton wouldn't have been at all surprised to see flames shooting out of his mouth.

"I will suck your eyeballs out, then tear you apart one limb at a time for disturbing me!" he sneered, advancing toward Newton, his Royal Court flanking him.

Acting on instinct, seething from the injustice that Herbert was dead, Newton reached into his knapsack and in one swift movement, like a gunfighter drawing a pistol, pulled out his flashlight. He aimed it at Prince Natas's feet, holding the flashlight with both hands to steady the trembling beam. "Make one more move and I'll blow you into tomorrow with my Radon Atomizer!" Newton bluffed, masking his fear with a boldness that put Natas on guard. The Liveds had never seen a flashlight. What kind of weapon was this and how much would it hurt?

Newton knew that as soon as Natas discovered his bluff, he was a goner. His only hope was Gertrude. Quickly he turned to the princess. "The

Liveds have no intention of becoming allies. The only reason they're here is to trick you into surrendering your forests. I have seen their kingdom. Every last tree has been cut down and burned," he implored.

"Is this true?" Gertrude asked, looking from Newton to Prince Natas. She didn't know whom or what to believe.

Natas let out a roar. "You are not even worthy to breathe the same air as a Lived! Who are you to accuse me?"

Oddly, the louder Natas ranted and raved, the more he reminded Newton of his brothers and the less scary he became. In spite of all his threats, Prince Natas didn't seem so tough.

That is, until the flashlight conked out.

This was an instance of colossal bad timing. Natas and Newton stood poised for a moment before they realized that their fortunes had changed.

Then Natas let out a great roar. "Killl himmm nowww!"

Newton closed his eyes and tensed his body, knowing that it was useless to resist. He hoped that it would be over quickly and painlessly (having his eyes sucked out was something he didn't want to experience while still conscious).

The attack never came. Instead, the Merriwarts, as if on cue, finally understood the Liveds for who they were. They rushed forward.

The battle was on! Shouts, punches, cries and bites filled the banquet hall. Though the Liveds were clearly outnumbered, they were better (and dirtier) fighters. However, the Merriwarts had an advantage that should not be underestimated: they fought with their hearts. Urged on by the shrieks of Gertrude (who skillfully threw uppercuts and head-butted Liveds with the fury of a tornado), the Merriwarts refused to back down. Knowing that if they lost their kingdom their way of life would be forever destroyed, what they lacked in skill they made up for in passion.

Newton got involved in the fray early, trying to trip Liveds, but soon realized that a boy among giants is a dangerous proposition. He wisely crawled to the back of the Great Hall near the doors, pressed himself against a wall and watched the fight. He knew that things could go either way. Merriwart bodies were flying everywhere, though the Liveds too were taking a beating. Much to his relief, the Merriwarts eventually overcame all but one Lived—Prince Natas.

. . . Who had been swinging from a chandelier,

knocking unsuspecting Merriwarts over by viciously kicking them in their backs. When he saw that he was the last Lived standing, Natas climbed up to a balcony, out of reach.

"Come down here at once, you coward, and surrender," Gertrude screamed.

"Ha! The fight has only begun. That was a warm-up," Natas replied. He stuck two fingers in his mouth and pierced the air with a whistle.

The hall went instantly quiet. Natas laughed. "Fools! In seconds, hundreds of Liveds will storm the hall and kill all of you!"

Newton knew that if what Natas said was true, the Merriwarts were done for. It had taken all they had to subdue the thirteen members of the Lived Royal Court.

If hundreds arrived . . .

Silence hung in the air like a disease. Natas stood on the balcony with a smug look on his evil face.

Agonizing seconds turned into minutes as all ears listened for the troops. Slowly, Natas's smile faded. Newton could see that he was wondering where his reinforcements were. Why hadn't they come on his signal?

"There are no troops," Gertrude declared. "Capture him!"

Natas swung back onto the chandelier and dropped to the ground. "I will never surrender!" he wailed, and fled toward the door. In a mad dash to avoid capture he zigged and zagged, as slippery as Vaseline.

Newton watched Natas in horror, desperately trying to think of a way to stop him. He would never be able to close the doors in time (even if he had the strength). Newton scanned the banquet hall, looking for something, anything.

Then he saw it. Coiled beside the door was a huge rope. Newton ran over and looped one end to the leg of a bench, then dragged the rope across the aisle, scrambled up the bench and tied the other end to the armrest.

Natas came barreling toward the door and hit the rope. He flew into the air, arms outstretched like a diver's, then landed hard on the ground. The Merriwarts pounced on the fallen Natas in what looked like a world record pileup. Though Natas still screamed and threatened, everyone knew the battle was won.

Chapter 14

The Kingdom of the Merriwarts had been saved!

Newton slumped to the ground, spent from moving the massive rope, happy that a lifetime on the losing end of the quadruplets' devious ways had taught him a thing or two about the art of tripping. Dazed Merriwarts slowly looked around, silently taking in the scene. The fallen Liveds were not moving.

After the Liveds were all tied up, with knots so complicated they would take years to undo, Gertrude walked over to Herbert and gently placed a hand on his shoulder. Everyone was silent and looking guilty with regret, for not one of them had spoken in Herbert's defense or helped him.

"I am so sorry you never lived to see how you saved our kingdom," Gertrude said, then began to weep. Her tears started a chain reaction of blubbering so that soon there wasn't a dry Merriwart eye in the hall. As the floor became more and more slippery with sadness and regret, Newton got up and walked toward Herbert.

He hovered over Herbert, overcome with emotion, unsure how to pay his last respects. Herbert was gone and Newton couldn't remember ever being sadder. Herbert was the first person he had known who died.

Suddenly Herbert's left eye opened. It looked around cautiously. Newton was confused. *Dead giants move their eyes?*

"We did it!" Herbert whispered, then smiled a painful smile.

It took Newton a moment to figure out he wasn't dreaming, that dead giants can't talk, and if Herbert was talking . . .

Newton jumped on Herbert, hugging him and shouting, "You're alive again!"

When the Merriwarts realized that Herbert wasn't dead, the room went from sadness to gladness to outright ecstasy. Their hero was alive enough to enjoy the victory party!

It was during the forty-seventh verse of "For He's a Jolly Good Fellow!" that Joe and Dr. Doosler drove back into the Great Hall. They had to rear-end Newton's heel a few times before he finally noticed them.

"Where's my medal?" Joe demanded after Newton picked up the Jeep, shouting over the noise of the celebration. "And one for Birdy Doosler as well."

"What are you talking about?" Newton asked.

It took a while but eventually Newton (along with Gertrude and Herbert) heard the story of how Joe and Dr. Doosler played their part in saving the day. Discovering that instead of water, the carts were filled with troops ready to spring out at Natas's whistle, the pair jimmied each and every release lock so it wouldn't open. As a result, when Natas whistled, the Lived warriors were trapped inside, unable to storm the banquet hall as planned. "You should have heard the banging!" Joe laughed. "What a colossal tactical blunder! I mean, come on, everyone knows about the Trojan Horse! It's so B.C.!"

"And to think I let that brute lick my toes."

Gertrude shuddered. "What would we have done without your help?"

"A soldier's duty is a soldier's duty." Joe shrugged, from his perch on Gertrude's nose. "But, Princess G., I sure will feel a lot better once the enemy has been relocated to a more secure locale."

Because Merriwarts were a peaceful race, they didn't have jails or anywhere to put an entire kingdom of Liveds.

Everyone was stumped for a solution until Newton spoke. "I have an idea," he said, pulling out his portal map. "We can send them to a place so barren, so desolate, so miserable that jail would look like paradise."

"Sounds horribly perfect," Gertrude replied. "Where is it?"

"We can send them home. Trust me, nothing could be worse than their own kingdom."

Instantly the princess agreed that this was a truly deserving fate for the ruthless Liveds. And so, cart by cart, the Merriwarts deposited the Liveds into the portal that would return them to their bleak existence.

They also rounded up the Liveds from the wedding party. Natas was the last Lived to be put inside. In spite of his current situation, the embarrassment of the flashlight and all the Merriwarts surrounding the portal, Natas still tried to act tough. He ranted and raged, spewed and sputtered. "We will come back and rip out your toenails one by one!" he cursed. "We haven't finished with you!"

"Oh, I think you have," Herbert calmly replied, and before Natas could utter another word, he slammed shut the portal door, almost clipping off the prince's fin in the process.

To erase the threat of the Liveds ever reentering the kingdom, the elders chanted the "Sealing Song," an off-key spell that made scalps tingle and arm hairs stand at attention, and permanently closed the portal.

A cloud-rattling cheer went up and the Merriwarts banged into one anothers' chests with joyful abandon. Newton, Joe and Dr. Doosler wisely didn't engage in the activity. Gertrude raised her pinky finger and sneezed (the royal symbol for an announcement). Immediately the flushed Merriwarts sneezed back and settled down, though the ground still rumbled with aftershocks of their activity.

"Do I ever feel like an idiot—" Gertrude began, but she was drowned out by objections from her subjects, who shouted, *"No!" "Not you!" "But you're so wise, so pretty!"*

Gertrude sneezed again. "It's true. I have been foolish. We've all been foolish—and look where it got us. We were so blind to promises of water that we never saw the evil that was staring us straight in the eyes. If it weren't for the heroic deeds of a few individuals, our kingdom would be kaput. Would Commander Joe, Newton and Herbert please step forward."

Newton picked up the Jeep, Herbert picked up Newton, and they faced the princess. The elders, who were usually advised on royal matters, muttered to themselves that they had no idea what the princess was planning.

Gertrude leaned over and looked at Joe. "Thanks to your quick thinking, the Lived troops never had a chance to attack. Clearly you know a thing or two about war. We would be honored if you would accept the post of Official Military Consultant for the kingdom. Even though we are a peaceful people, we don't ever want to be caught off-guard again"

"Is it a paid position?"

"No," Gertrude replied, not in the least offended. "Merriwarts don't have money. But take heart, there's no limit on the number of orders you're allowed to issue."

Joe decided not to point out that he didn't have a heart. Instead he asked, "What kind of orders?"

"Any kind you feel like, I suppose," she said and handed him a tiny megaphone. "Use this so we can all hear you."

There wasn't a *Commander* in front of Joe's name for nothing—bossing people around was what he liked to do best. "Since my needs are simple and I've never held an official title, I'll take it. One condition, though: Dr. Doosler is my Chief of Staff in case I get tied up with a mission somewhere else," Joe said boldly, but backed down a bit by adding quickly, "Of course, if that's all right with you *and* Dr. Doosler."

Both agreed, and Joe became the Official Military Consultant. He started ordering everyone into formation for the rest of Gertrude's announcements, but Newton advised him to wait until tomorrow before plunging into the job. Joe agreed.

Next Gertrude addressed Newton. "After witnessing your bravery in front of Natas, nothing I can say will ever repay our debt to you. Before anyone else, you realized how much trouble we were in and risked your life to save us."

Newton blushed, and then, because Gertrude didn't say anything for a few moments, he wondered if that was going to be it. But Gertrude, notoriously absentminded, was nudged back on track by one of the elders. "Oh yes, where were we? Newton, as a reward, from this day on, you are an official member of the Kingdom of the Merriwarts. As such, you will be entitled to full benefits and privileges." Murmurs of approval swept through the crowd. Newton a Merriwart! Unprecedented! Never in their history had the honor been bestowed on a foreigner.

Gertrude then added the best part of all. "Of course, as a Merriwart, you will have your very own tree fort!" Newton felt like a lifetime of Christmases had been heaped on him, he was so happy. Finally, a place to set up his inventions away from the quadruplets' grubby hands! Before he had a chance to thank Gertrude, Newton was lifted up and passed from giant to giant. Each Merriwart licked him (slobbering was their way of welcoming him into the community). Newton was thoroughly and disgustingly slimed by the time Gertrude spoke to Herbert.

The giant stood nervously before his ravishing princess. "Firstly, Herbert, we owe you a sincere apology for not believing what you said about the Liveds and not coming to your defense when they attacked you. Secondly, because of your bravery,

you are no longer banished. And finally, for your heroic part in saving our kingdom, for your acts of bravery, I am bestowing upon you the Order of Merriwart Knighthood!"

The crowd *oohed* and *aahed* as Herbert knelt and bent his head. Merriwart Knighthood, Newton later learned, was a rare honor that, in the past two hundred years, only one other Merriwart had received.

As Gertrude recited the Knight's Code and lightly tapped Herbert's shoulders eighteen times (a tap for each of the knightly virtues), Newton saw

Herbert struggling not to get choked up. The giant was so happy that tears squeezed out, in spite of his noble efforts to dam up the waters. Newton felt himself going a little mushy with pride.

As Herbert stood up from the ceremony, his fellow Merriwarts bowed deeply to pay their respects.

Perhaps it was because his brain had gone mushy from Gertrude's praise that Herbert decided to do what he did. He fished into his pocket and brought out the wooden engagement ring he had long ago given up hope of ever putting on the finger of his beloved. Clearing his throat (which required a bit of effort considering all the gunk that was up there from his efforts not to cry), Herbert asked simply, "Gertrude, will you marry me?"

Herbert once had told Newton that if he ever had the chance to propose to Gertrude it would be with a long speech, flowery words, and promises of heroic deeds, never-ending love and a lifetime of baked goods. After hearing Herbert's simple proposal, Newton agreed that in the end, it made more sense to just come right out and say what he had to say, plain and simple.

Before the elders could interject and remind everyone that princesses never marry common Merriwarts (even if they are knights), Gertrude jumped onto Herbert, threw her arms around him and cried, "I do!! I do! I *do!*" (three times, just in case anybody was hard of hearing) and started eagerly licking the inside of his ear. This prompted Joe to comment, "Right now, if I had a stomach, and if that stomach had food in it, I'd barf." The Merriwarts bounced up and down with approval, for they realized that if someone like Herbert could marry royalty, well then, the possibilities for the rest of them were endless.

After cleaning out Herbert's eardrums, Gertrude climbed up on his shoulders. "I have an announcement," she began. "Tonight at midnight this hunka-hunka gorgeous giant and I will tie the knot."

Herbert walked over to Newton (still with Gertrude on his shoulders). "Newton, will you be my best man?" he asked.

"I'm just a kid."

"Then, will you be my best kid?"

"Do I have to get dressed up?"

"Nope. In fact, it's customary to get dressed down at our weddings."

"Then, I'd be honored, Herbert. Though I want you to know, I would have been your best man no matter what I had to wear."

Herbert forgot he was carrying Gertrude when he bent down to shake Newton's hand, and the princess toppled over.

Being tossed off her future husband made the princess practically pass out.

It was either from the glee, or from the alarming bump on her head.

Chapter 15

The bride and groom had gone to get ready for the wedding. Newton had wanted to climb up to his brand-new, very own tree fort before the wedding, but he was so popular, his presence so in demand that sleeping was out of the question—it would have been considered very rude. Once word spread that Newton had visited a couple of Merriwart homes, invitations flooded in like Valentine cards to a pretty girl. So from tree fort to tree fort Newton *boink-boink-boinked*, at each stop drinking a tankard of Bliss (the Merriwart national drink) and being encouraged to describe in excruciating detail the wretched conditions of the Lived caves.

Later, when he finally returned to his fort Newton was halfway to a wicked case of laryngitis from talking and more tired than he could remember being.

Newton lay down and was sure he would pass out immediately, but he started thinking about home. Though he hated to admit it, he missed everyone—even the quadruplets.

Commander Joe and Dr. Doosler drove up in the Jeep and interrupted his thoughts. "Where have you been, Pokey? Birdy Doosler has been brewing up some ideas that she'd like to run by you."

"As previously mentioned, Dr. Doosler can speak for herself," Dr. Doosler said.

"Right. Sorry. It's just that Dr. Doosler was trying to figure out a way to fix the Merriwarts' water problem."

"And you want to do this right now?" Newton asked, wondering if his eyelid muscles would break from staying up so long.

"No, yesterday. Of course *now*, Pokey. Wouldn't that be a heck of a wedding gift to give them?"

"I suppose so . . ." Newton replied uncertainly,

thinking they had done plenty for the Merriwarts already. "Where do I come in?"

"We've been surveying and have already sniffed out an underground water source. What we need from you are schematic diagrams. A system. A plan. Nothing too complicated, just an invention of staggering simplicity."

About to protest that he had no energy, Newton thought about it for a moment and decided problem-solving would tickle his brain much more than sleeping. And he had always read that a change was as good as a rest. This would be a good time to run an experiment on that idea as well.

With Dr. Doosler's help, it didn't take Newton long to devise a solution. Using basic $e=mc^2$ formulations, quantum physics and eureka shortcuts known only to top-notch inventors, they devised an intricate system of pulleys, weights and counter-levers. While Newton and Dr. Doosler completed the schematic drawings, Joe mobilized the Merriwarts with the efficiency of a field general hoping for a promotion. No one dared disobey the Official Military Consultant.

And by evening, buckets of water were being hauled up through the branches, replenishing the kingdom's depleted supplies. To the technologically challenged Merriwarts, the device was nothing short of miraculous, ensuring their prosperity for generations.

As a result everyone was in high spirits by midnight. The banquet hall was once again packed, but instead of the somber mood the Liveds had cast over the earlier ceremony, there was chatting, laughing, awful-joke telling and the drinking of Herculean quantities of Bliss.

The bride and groom were married and in doing so said lots of mushy things about each other and of course exchanged gooey kisses and even gooier licks. Newton was particularly disgusted with the toe-licking ceremony. There was dancing, juggling, more Bliss-drinking, eating (Herbert made a spectacular Slamberry Pie) and toasting to good health, long life and beauty warts. Newton was told he was an outstanding best man and that he performed wonderfully all of his duties (including the peculiar custom of rubbing bellies with Herbert).

Aside from the bride and groom, perhaps no one had more fun at the wedding than Rose. Herbert had not forgotten about her—especially after she had restored the portal map. He understood Rose's crime was no worse than his Meal of Seduction and convinced Gertrude and the elders that she didn't deserve to be banished. Not only was his recommendation wholeheartedly agreed upon, but once Rose returned and demonstrated a little hocus-pocus, it was decided that she should be appointed the Official Merriwart Wizard—a position that had gone unfilled for a thousand years because the last wizard mistakenly (and irreversibly) transformed himself into a boulder before he had a chance to train a successor. In spite of Herbert's efforts to convince her otherwise, Rose attended the wedding naked. The guests pretended not to notice or stare at inappropriate places because secretly they were afraid of offending her and worried she might put a hex on them.

When the sun was starting to peek over the horizon signaling that a new day was under way, the party was still in full swing (literally, as Merriwarts boinked through the trees). Newton had long ago fallen asleep in a corner and was rudely awoken by Joe driving up in the Jeep and repeatedly ramming into his forehead.

Newton, who couldn't remember the last time he had slept so deeply, reluctantly opened his eyes.

"What? Couldn't you see I was busy?" he said testily.

Joe ignored the cranky tone. "Good morning to you too. Pokey, Dr. Doosler has been summoned back to Jupiter and wanted to say goodbye."

"I look forward to doing business with you in the future," Dr. Doosler said, and handed Newton a tiny business card. "This is my portal address. If you ever find the schematic diagrams for your wings, we should talk. An invention like that has universal sales potential."

"Thanks," Newton replied, now sitting up. He tucked the card in his pocket.

"Close your eyes again, Newton," Joe ordered.

Newton was now fully awake. "Why? I'm up."

"*Do it!*" Joe ordered.

Newton pretended to close them, but really he could see everything—especially the part when Commander Joe lip-smacked Dr. Doosler with a wet kiss. As soon as Joe stepped out of the Jeep, Dr. Doosler drove off at hyper-speed.

"You can look, Newton," Joe said, staring wistfully after Dr. Doosler. "If I had a heart, I could fall in love with a woman like that."

Newton, extremely embarrassed by all the

lovey-dovey, kept quiet until Joe snapped out of his googly-eyed, moon-faced silliness and barked, "What's the plan, Pokey?"

"Maybe it's about time we too headed home. What do you think?"

"Well, I am Official Military Consultant, but for the moment our work here is done. I suppose I could use a little R and R."

Newton and Joe found Herbert with Gertrude, arm in arm, watching the sunrise, licking each other's necks.

"All right, you two, cut it out! Lips at attention! That's an order!" Joe shouted through his megaphone.

Herbert and Gertrude turned, saw Joe and stuck their tongues out before breaking into giggles.

Joe shook his head wearily. "Young love," he sighed.

Newton decided not to mention what he had seen between Joe and Dr. Doosler.

"What's up, Newton?" Herbert asked after he had stopped laughing.

"Joe and I are going home."

Gertrude protested. "But you can't! The party has just begun. There's still another month left!"

It took Newton a while to finally convince them that he must leave, that he had to return to his life if there was any hope of passing fifth grade.

"Well, in that case," Herbert said, "it won't take me more than a few minutes to pack my bags and get ready."

Gertrude, who knew about Herbert's promise to help Newton with his bullying brothers, urged him to hurry. "How long do you think he'll be gone?" she asked. "I'm missing him already."

"Well, that's the thing. Not very long. In fact, he won't be gone at all," Newton replied, then turned to Herbert. "I've decided to go back alone. Don't take this the wrong way—it's not that I don't want your help, it's just that I'd feel awful taking you away from Gertrude so early in the marriage."

Herbert gasped and his eyeballs bulged. "What about your brothers? What about stopping them from bullying you? I don't mind terrorizing them, honestly I don't."

"You know, after facing the Liveds, the quadruplets don't seem nearly so tough." The idea of having a giant scare the quadruplets into leaving him alone was tempting, but deep down Newton realized that if he was ever going to do all the great things he had planned in his life (exploring Mars, inventing a money machine, discovering a cure for homework), he'd need the full use of his entire brain. Part of it couldn't be occupied with worrying that his brothers would restart their harassment as soon as Herbert wasn't around. No, he'd face them himself and live (or die) with the consequences.

Herbert could see by the angle of Newton's jaw that there was no point in arguing. The kid's mind was made up. "Are you really going back?"

"Yeah. The longer I stay, the harder it's going to be to go."

"You're sure you couldn't wait a couple of years?" Herbert asked. It was obvious he had grown alarmingly fond of Newton. Herbert's bottom lip quivered like he might bawl, but since he was now important, he held back the tears. "I remember the first time I saw you in the attic . . ."

Newton rubbed Herbert's shin. "Don't worry. I'll visit. In fact, I'll be here so much, you'll probably start getting sick of me."

"Oh, no, Newton. We'd never get sick of you. We'll reopen the attic portal so you can come back whenever you want," Gertrude said, then bent over and gave him a kiss. Joe, sensing he might be next, ordered the princess not to touch him.

Newton wiped off his face. "Speaking of attics, before I go, Herbert, there's one thing I'm still confused about. When I first saw you roaming around in my attic, what were you looking for?"

Herbert blushed. "Um . . . well . . . you see. . ." He stalled. "It's like this . . . I know this is going to sound foolish. . ."

"Out with it!" commanded Joe.

Reluctantly Herbert answered. "I was searching for the Meal of Seduction's final ingredient."

Gertrude arched her eyebrow. "Which was . . . ?" she asked, trying to act offended, but everyone could tell she was just pretending.

"One smelly, crusty, human sock. The portal map indicated your bedroom was a breeding ground full of them."

"But you never made it there. Without the sock, how were you able to cook the meal?"

Herbert blushed again. "That's the funny thing. Margaret thought . . . well, no that's not true . . . I asked Margaret . . . actually, I told Margaret . . . okay, okay, I ordered Margaret to borrow one from you when she flew you back that night."

Then Newton remembered. Of course. When he

woke up, he couldn't figure out why he was missing a sock when his shoe was still on his foot. Now it all made sense.

"I'm sorry, Newton. I'm not a thief. It's just that I was desperate."

"Herbert, it's all right. Everyone knows socks are meant to be lost. That's why they always give you two instead of one."

Though Newton tried to convince Gertrude and Herbert to let him and Joe slip away unnoticed, they absolutely would not allow it. And so, by the time they stepped into the portal, the entire Merriwart kingdom had gathered for the send-off. Young and old, they had come to say goodbye to the boy who had saved their forest. When Gertrude gave the signal (pulling her left earlobe), the Merriwarts began jumping up and down as if they were on invisible pogo sticks, and hummed his name over and over again.

"What's going on?" Joe, who was tucked in Newton's front pocket, asked.

"I don't know, but it's making me tingle. Especially my toes."

"Me too."

The Merriwart Buzz-Buzz-Hop-Along had the effect of making Newton feel peaceful, proud and overflowing with happiness all at the same time. In short, it was the best goodbye he had ever had.

And then the portal closed.

Chapter 16

Newton was still tingling when the portal deposited him and Joe in the attic. Peering down through the opening, he could not believe what he saw. His room was almost empty. Everything, except for a few boxes and some dust balls, had been removed. His pictures, his books, his telescope, his rug, his bed—gone. It was as if he had never lived there, as if he had been wiped out.

The quadruplets were busy moving boxes and didn't notice Newton's head poking out from the hole in the ceiling.

The wonderful feeling Newton had had a few

moments ago in the Kingdom of the Merriwarts vanished. "What are you doing?" he managed to sputter.

At the sound of his voice, the quadruplets instantly dropped their boxes. *Smash!* It sounded like Earl had shattered Newton's experiment beakers and Ernest destroyed the photography equipment. But all Newton saw were the contents that spilled out of Engelbert's box. His journals—including #22, which contained the notes and schematic diagrams for the wings!

The quadruplets turned their shocked faces toward Newton.

"I said, what are you doing?" Newton repeated, calmly.

"So, you're alive. But don't think we're not turning your room into a racquetball court. Mom and Dad are so out of it worrying about you, we decided to do a little rearranging. Since you hadn't been home for two days and hadn't completed even one single job on their list, we just assumed you must be dead," Engelbert said. "Now, get down here right now so we can beat you up."

"They didn't send anyone out to look for me?"

"Of course they did. They cried and moaned, but we told them to face the facts. You'd most likely run away from home or been hit by a car!" Engelbert said. "And by the way, we saw you slide under home plate and almost wreck the game for us. Luckily the Owls still won, but we also owe you a lesson for that little incident."

Eight beady eyes stared up at Newton. They smoldered without a trace of love, and Newton wondered why he had been so quick to leave the Merriwarts.

"What's the plan, Pokey?" Joe whispered.

"The Cannonball."

"You sure?"

"I'm sure," Newton replied, but of course, he wasn't the least bit sure.

"Why are you mumbling into your pocket?" Earl asked suspiciously. "You better not be walkie-talkie-ing for backup."

Newton was about to say he wasn't, but instead jumped through the attic opening and knocked over the quadruplets like dominos. They'd been so surprised that their younger brother hadn't tried to escape that they hadn't expected the human cannon.

Engelbert was the first to recover. He sprang up and grabbed Newton. "You'll pay for that!"

"Then, bill me!" Newton replied as he watched

his other three brothers groggily stand up. "I'm ready and waiting. Whatever you're going to do, do it now."

"Or what?" Ernest threatened.

"Or nothing," Newton replied. "Just get it over with. I don't care. I'm sick of running from you four. I'm sick of being blamed for everything. I'm sick of always feeling afraid. You're nothing but bullies. So here I am, bully away."

Again the quadruplets were shocked. This wasn't how it was supposed to work. Their younger brother was supposed to run away, shriek in terror, do everything in his power to avoid their evil clutches. Clearly there had to be something behind his new strategy.

"Search him!" Engelbert ordered.

Newton had no idea what they expected to find. During their pat-down they snuck in a few punches, some bruise-producing pinches and a couple of well-placed bites, but otherwise nothing too serious. They also didn't find Commander Joe.

But in his back pocket they found the portal map.

Engelbert held it up like a trophy. "What do we have here?" he asked smugly.

"It's a portal map. I wouldn't open it if I were you," Newton warned, remembering Witch

Hazel's instructions that the consequences of anyone older than eleven looking at the map would be disastrous.

"And why not?" Engelbert leered.

"Your imaginations probably couldn't handle it. I was told it wouldn't be a good idea."

"Well, whoever said that is an even bigger fool than you."

Newton shrugged. Arguing with the quadruplets was about as effective as teaching a dog Latin.

Unconcerned by Newton's warning, the brothers huddled around as Engelbert slowly unrolled the map.

At first nothing happened, though they were completely fascinated by the portal openings. Then slowly the color left the quadruplets' faces, their eyes opened wide, wider, then widest as a look of complete terror overcame them. Newton wondered if somehow the portal map made them see their own souls.

Then it started. At first in wisps, then in entire clumps, their hair began falling out, piling at their feet like snow. Soon not one strand remained (eyebrow or otherwise).

As if directed by a symphony conductor, four voices rose in a horrifying screech.

The wail made Newton's teeth vibrate. He put his hands over his ears.

Mr. and Mrs. Wiggins raced up the stairs. . .

Only to discover their beautiful, kind, smart boys were . . . *bald!*

And Newton had returned. "Newton Wiggins, you're back!" they shouted, and hugged him.

Newton was surprised. *His mom and dad actually loved him! Who would have believed it!* That great feeling from the Kingdom of the Merriwarts came right back, all because of a bear-size hug from his parents. It

seemed they would never let go, and Newton never wanted to be let go.

Then it happened. A speechless Engelbert poked at his father until the hug broke up—and held out the map. And before Newton could intercept or warn his parents not to look, it was too late. Exactly the same thing happened (although his father was already going bald and didn't have nearly as much hair to lose).

Suddenly his parents were no longer concerned with Newton. So caught up was everyone in rubbing their heads and staring at each other, Newton went unnoticed. His mother looked like an alien and his brothers like overgrown babies. His father looked like himself, only more so.

"What are we going to do!" Earl asked.

"This is disastrous!" Engelbert cried. "Everyone will laugh!"

"I can't go to the curling bonspiel without hair! I'll never be allowed to skip!" his mother moaned.

"I've got an idea!" his father said. "We'll drive to the cottage and hide out until it grows back!"

And with that, the six of them scurried off to pack their bags. In less time than it takes to toast a slice of bread, they had piled in the car and were backing out the driveway.

Without even bothering to toot the horn goodbye to Newton or tell him to eat the rest of the lasagna in the freezer.

Nope, they had completely and utterly forgotten about him.

Sadly Newton watched them disappear down the street. He knew the portal map had made them lose their perspective entirely. Their poor imaginations!

"Well, Pokey, then there were two," Joe said, popping out from Newton's shirt. "Your family is an awfully odd bunch. No offense, of course."

"None taken. Sometimes it sure seems that way," Newton sighed. "But they hugged me."

"Yeah, I know. That was some squeeze. First class. Thought I was going to pass out," Joe said. He paused, then added, "It's true, you know—they really do care about you, even if they are completely weird."

"I know," Newton replied, and for the first time in his life, he really, truly, absolutely did know that his parents loved him.

Not sure what else to do, Newton trudged down to the basement and began the long process of hauling the contents of his bedroom back upstairs. It took hours.

That night for dinner, instead of lasagna, Newton

made a marshmallow-and-peanut-butter sandwich. After rereading his old journals he was finally ready for bed. Joe had long ago crawled back into his old cigar box and gone to sleep.

As Newton tucked himself in, he couldn't help but think about the Merriwarts and wonder what his friends were doing. Even though he still had Joe for company, Newton was lonely.

He turned off the light and started to drift into dreamland.

Newton heard a tap on the window. At first he ignored it, figuring it was just the branches knocking against the glass. However, when he opened his eyes, he saw a silhouette of a head and shoulders in the moonlight.

Who could possibly be lurking outside his bedroom at this time of night? If it was a robber, Newton wished the thief would just break in quietly and not disturb him. No matter how hard he tried, attempting to sleep with a potential ax-murderer at the window proved impossible, so Newton shone his flashlight at the intruder.

Instantly Max's face lit up like a pumpkin.

The deserter had returned! The disbeliever was back! Newton definitely didn't want to see his ex–best friend and did the mature thing by pulling the covers over his head and pretending to go back to sleep. But Max was as persistent as a headache and kept rapping—*rat-a-tat-tat*—against the glass until Newton had no choice but to open the window.

"Where have you been?" Max asked, standing on a ladder. "I've called and called, but no one answered. Then your parents crashed their car into my mom's station wagon and didn't even wait around. Did you know they're bald? They said something about going to the cottage until they were better."

"I've just been busy," Newton replied vaguely. "What do you want?"

"Are you going to let me in or what? I'm getting frostbite."

Newton hesitated.

"Come on, Newton. Please. There's something I want to tell you."

Against his better judgment Newton let him in.

Once inside, Max paced the room for a couple of minutes as Newton watched him warily. Whatever was on his mind, he sure was taking a long time to spit it out. When Max finally started talking, his apology came out in a rush. "I don't know how to say this, Newton, except to say I'm sorry. I let you down, which was bad enough, but during a mission, well, that's beyond excusable. I don't know if I'll ever forgive myself. I wasn't there for you when you needed me. What kind of soldier does a thing like that? I feel like a heel. I could kick myself. I haven't been able to eat . . ." Max went on and on, describing the thousands of push-ups he had done to punish himself, the letters he wrote, how he was the awfulest friend in the entire universe. When Newton could not bear to listen to one more word of Max apologizing he cut him off.

"All right, all right. I get the idea. You're forgiven. Forget it."

Max went on for another moment before actually hearing what Newton had said. "I am?" he asked, barely able to believe Newton had let him off so easily. "Really?"

"Really," Newton replied.

"Are we still best friends?" Max asked timidly.

"We'll always be best friends." For a moment Newton thought Max might hug him, but of course that would have led to a lot of awkwardness.

Instead, to prove that they were still friends, Max punched Newton in the arm and then let Newton punch him back just a little harder, without complaining.

As Max rubbed his shoulder, Newton asked what had made him change his mind.

"I visited Witch Hazel and drank the Ogre Brew. After that, I knew exactly what you were talking about," Max replied. "Oh, I almost forgot, where's Commander Joe?"

"Over there," Newton said, pointing to the cigar box Joe was sleeping in.

Max opened it and tickled Joe a couple of times in the stomach. "It's me, Max," Max said when Joe opened his eyes.

"I know who it is. I thought you didn't believe toys can talk?"

"I was wrong. I brought something for you." Reaching into his pocket, Max pulled out a plastic arm and handed it to Joe.

Instead of thanking him, Joe took one look at the limb and gasped. "Torturer!" he shouted.

Max hadn't expected this reaction but immediately saw the misunderstanding. "Oh, no. You've got it wrong. I special-ordered it from the company. It didn't come from another toy. I would never do that."

Joe examined Max suspiciously. "That's the truth? Because I could not wear an arm knowing some defenseless action figure had been mutilated."

After Max crossed his heart and triple-reassured him that no toys had been hurt in the obtaining of the arm, Joe lay down for the reattachment operation. "Sock it to me," Joe said, then chuckled. "Get it? *Socket*, sock it! That's funny. You fellows can use it if you want."

Though Max had mistakenly ordered another right arm instead of a left, Joe didn't mind one bit. "It's all *right*," he joked, then proceeded to do nine hundred and ninety-nine one-armed push-ups before declaring the limb A-1 certified.

While Joe was busy testing out his new arm, Max asked Newton if he wanted to stay at his house until his parents came back. "My mom said to tell you that I'd sleep on the floor and you could have my bed. She also said if you came, she'd make elephant-ear doughnuts." Max paused. "Don't take this the wrong way, but sometimes I wonder if my mom actually likes you more than she likes me."

"Really?"

"Maybe."

Newton looked around at his messy room. "That'd be nice. I don't think I like it much in this big house with just Commander Joe."

And so Newton and Max (along with Joe) climbed down the ladder into the night. Along the way to Max's house they invented all kinds of histories for the ghosts, ghouls and spirits that they passed, and who passed through them.

When they neared Max's, they could see that the light was on in the kitchen and Mrs. Brown was awake doing the crossword, waiting for her son's safe return.

As they walked up the path toward the back door, Newton was thinking, in spite of all that had happened, how happy he was. For the first time in a long time—since he could remember, in fact—he wasn't scared of something or dreading someone. *He had stood up to the quadruplets!* That made him feel downright delirious. Well, that and the reaction his parents had had when they realized he was alive. Newton knew that when his family eventually returned, in spite of their sometimes mean and definitely odd ways, he'd be glad to go home. For now, he didn't mind bunking down with Max.

Max paused before opening the door. "What do you want to do tomorrow?" he asked.

"I don't know. Why?"

"Well, maybe, if you feel like it, we could go exploring."

"On an adventure?" Newton asked. "Seriously?"

"Oh, I'd understand, considering everything

you've been through, if you weren't up to it. But they're saying it's supposed to rain all day."

Newton hesitated, and then a smile slowly worked its way across his face. "Sure. Why not? I could show you my Merriwart tree fort, and in the afternoon, if we have time, there's a person on Jupiter I'd like you to meet."